The Preacher's Wife

Sa'id Salaam

Published by Black Ink Publications, 2020.

THE PREACHER'S WIFE

First edition. April 12, 2020.

Written by Sa'id Salaam.

Prologue

How the hell did I get here? Teresa wondered inwardly as she glanced up at the giggling teenager standing over her.

If the act wasn't sad enough, she also had to contend with the young man's vulgar speech and sweaty balls slapping at her chin.

"Dats right! Suck dat dick bitch! Eat it hoe!" Lil Red demanded as he humped her face. Technically it couldn't be called a blow job because the vile little boy was literally fucking her face.

Teresa gagged loudly each time he slammed into her larynx. Her full mouth forced her to inhale the flavor of nuts that had missed at least two showers, and in the sweltering Atlanta heat that's not a good idea.

"Just hurry," Teresa sighed, *"And do not... cu.... Ewww! He's coming in my mouth!"*

"Mmm take it bitch! Eat! Eat!" Lil Red giggled as he skeeted on her tonsils. Teresa had no choice but to swallow the pulses of bitter semen since her head was held firmly in place.

"Dayum you got some fire ass head!" The man child exclaimed, taking a few final humps before extracting himself from her mouth.

"Thank you, you're too kind," Teresa replied sarcastically but the quip was wasted on the ignorant young dealer.

"Here you go shawty," Lil Red said, extending his open palm filled with dime size pieces of crack. The young veteran had cut the drug at angles that made it appear more than it actually was. Still, five dimes was a lot for some head.

The local junkies will go as low as four dollars in a pinch. But this was no local junky. Her SUV, clothes, and even her smell spoke money, yet she had none. Lil Red didn't think she would accept his crass proposal to 'suck a nigga dick' but she did.

1

Teresa looked at the drugs with dismay. She felt like slapping the poison across the room. However, a far more intense urge insisted she plucked them from his hand.

"Shit fall through tomorrow, I'll let you suck this dick again," Lil Red offered politely over his shoulder as he exited the hotel room.

As soon as he crossed the threshold of the door, Teresa ran to secure it. She loathed the ghetto of Atlanta, but crack cocaine was not sold in her upscale suburban neighborhood.

She quickly removed one of the rocks from its tiny plastic bag and spilt it in two. After loading one half onto her straight shooter, she quickly followed it up with a flame.

'*Ahhh!*' Teresa exclaimed when she finally exhaled that overdue hit. She deserved it too for all she does. Daughter Hazel was at ballet class and son Calvin was at soccer, this was "me time".

Her free hours were spent devouring the drugs she purchased with her dignity. Then it was time to return to her life, "Life as the Preachers Wife."

Chapter 1

Teresa Sanders was born Teresa McCoy in Atlanta, at Grady Hospital thirty five Christmas days ago. Complications ensured she would be the couple's only child.

Her parents reigned over a mid-sized church on Atlanta's south west side. The first Baptist Church of Christ was located on busy Cascade Ave. The congregation consisted entirely of the middle class home owners in the area. They tithed generously to the church and to pastor McCoy personally.

They made sure he had a new car every year 'cuz pastor can't been seen driving no bullshit.' The church even gifted the family the biggest house in the area.

The income allowed the McCoy's to lavish their child with gifts and special treatment that spoiled the pretty little girl rotten. By three years old, Teresa was not only use having her way she actually demanded it.

"No" was a word totally foreign to the Prima Donna. She was prone to world class tantrums if not given her way. At times the brat would insist upon items she didn't really desire. This was done to ensure a garage laden with unwanted novelties that no longer held her interest.

Teresa was a beautiful baby, then a pretty little girl. By high school she was drop dead gorgeous. She even inherited her mom's wide hips and fat ass that had hooked her daddy many years back. Hands down she was the prettiest girl in any room she walked into.

Her parents enrolled her in all girls' schools in attempt to keep dicks out of their child. By high school they had enrolled her in a prestigious Christian Academy. The sky high tuition, they felt would keep the riff raff away. Yes, the McCoy's were naïve enough to believe money meant class and sophistication.

Why they thought this environment would be any safer morally than anywhere else is a mystery. Sure they were free from the violence

3

that plagues the inner city schools. However, all those sexually repressed girls in the same place was just as dangerous. It created a sexual energy comparable only to the sun.

Sex was the topic of the day, every day, and all day. There were even a few lesbian couples who dated discreetly. They figured same sex was better than no sex.

Most of the staff at the school was female. The idea was to create a no dick environment, a green zone if you will. The few males who did work there were filtered by unattractiveness and thoroughly screened. They all passed background checks, even Coach Jenkins.

Mathew Jenkins was a twenty three year old recent grad of a Bible college. He was a junior pastor at one of Atlanta's mega churches and had excellent references. His only flaw was being a hunk.

He was so handsome; he almost didn't get the job. Even the head administrator got a little moist during the interview. Finding no other, or no ugly suitable substitute male or female, Coach Jenkins was hired.

All the girls as well as half of the staff flirted shamelessly with the well-built P.E. instructor. Coach, however was far too upright pious and honest to return the interest shown to him. He was superman, until Teresa came along shaking her kryptonite.

"Lord have mercy!" He exclaimed when he saw Teresa stretching her hamstrings before class. The first things he noticed were her big brown legs. She looked like she could leap a building in a single bound.

A pretty morsel of ass-cheek protruded from the tiny school issued shorts. When she stood upright her full breast made the words "Christian Academy" on the shirt look like a billboard.

Not only was he hard as a diamond from gawking at the girl but found himself being propelled towards her.

"Excuse me young lady," he began cautiously, "When you stretch don't bounce. Slow.....and ..... Easy," he demonstrated.

"Oh okay, thanks!" Teresa gushed, thankful for the advice as well as a chance to see the man who had all the girls buzzing up close and personal.

"Like this?" she asked, as she slowly bent at the waist until she was touching her toes.

"Let me see," he said sliding behind her to get a good view of her round ass. "Perfect!"

The private lesson came to an abrupt end as the other girls began filing out the locker room. The session was over, but the last lustful gaze they shared said something else had begun. The seeds were sown.

Coach and student bantered playfully every chance they got. The mutual attraction grew into intense staring matches charged with sexual tones. It was now just a matter of time. The only thing keeping him out of the girl was opportunity. She was as good as fucked first chance he got.

Teresa was conflicted between her upbringing and her desires. She had fully intended on saving herself for her future husband, but now that was in question. Coach soaked her panties daily with his deep voice and brown eyes. The occasional brush against each other that they managed made her vagina throb.

She wasn't alone in her frustration. Coach had been an athlete in high school and had plenty of girls. Halfway through college he put his dick away picked up the Bible and vowed celibacy. Now he found himself masturbating after an encounter with the young stunner.

Yep, just a matter of time. Neither were surprised when a date was finally planned. It wasn't a date in the traditional sense. He would not come calling on her at home to meet the parents. They just arranged to be in the same place at the same time.

Totally harmless, right?

Chapter 2

Reverend McCoy was gifted a brand new Cadillac around the time of Teresa's extravagant sweet sixteen party. She frowned at the offer of his slightly used vehicle. She claimed that "it was so last years." Her doting father chided himself for being insensitive and quickly traded it in for a new convertible.

Even with her own car, Teresa's movements were still monitored closely. Her comings and goings were verified by phone and GPS. Dad knew his daughter was fine and saw the reactions men gave her. He even had to check a couple of deacons about looking at her ass.

Not to mention he was quite the dicks-man himself at that age. He bedded half the neighborhood including his, then sixteen year old, wife. Momma was a little easier to maneuver around, so that's who Teresa tried.

"Momma I'm fixing to go to the mall and meet up with some friends," Teresa sang, lying to her mother for the first time. Since she had such a stellar record her mother eagerly accepted the half-truth.

"Ok, have fun, drive safe and...?"

"No boys!" Teresa laughed

At least that part was true. Matthew was a man not a boy.

Teresa parked her car on the absolute outskirts of the malls huge parking lot. This was to give her a little privacy as she pulled off the loose fitting pants she wore and wiggled into the skin tight pair she brought along. She then pulled off the sweatshirt revealing the tight tee that revealed her breast.

A cursory check in the rearview mirror confirmed that her mid-back length hair was still perfect. Only then was the top lowered as she cruised around to the mall's valet parking to make her grand entrance.

Every male head turned as she sashayed into the mall. The attention was surprising as men married, single, young, old, straight and gay stared. A few of the younger more assertive guys made advances, but

6

they fell upon deaf ears. Teresa only had eyes for one man, and there he was at the food court right on time.

"Wow! You look great!" Coach exclaimed taking her hands and planting a kiss on her cheek. It was the first time a man had ever touched her causing her to flinch.

"I'm sorry," Matthew apologized fearfully as he misunderstood the reaction. "I... just..."

"No I'm fine! No problem, you look great too." Teresa smiled as she regained her composure. She wanted to go wring out her panties but didn't. Instead she tipped toed up and returned the gesture.

The plan was to catch the DOPE BOY movie at two o-clock so they headed to the mall's theater. With thirty minutes to spare coach led her into the arcade.

"Win me a prize!" Teresa demanded as she would her parents.

"Sure!" Mathew agreed eagerly. Just like her parents. He slid a dollar into the game releasing miniature basketballs. The athlete banked shot after shot into the small goal until the timer ran out.

"Here you try," He offered as a row of tickets slid out of the machine.

"I can't do that," Teresa giggled as her date guided her to the machine. She was far too prissy to shoot hoops but decided to try it for him.

Another dollar was inserted, releasing the balls and starting the timer. She missed every shot, getting more and more frustrated.

"Something must be wrong with the game!" she insisted, "It's either rigged or broken."

"No, it's your technique. Here, let me show you."

Like any coach he put his arms around her. He pressed his body against hers, his arms against hers, and helped her shoot hoops.

Teresa casually leaned her ass onto the erection slowly growing towards her and began gyrating. Even after the buzzer had sounded, announcing the end of the game, they lingered until an impatient adolescent demanded they move along.

Coach bought her everything she pointed at in the movie's concession stand. She had no plans on eating the majority of it but ordered it anyway. Once inside the darken theater she slipped her hand inside his.

Neither were able to fully concentrate on Killa Cam on the big screen, as they were both distracted by the others' hand. Even after the movie had ended they maintained their hand holding while they exited the mall. It wasn't until after the valet delivered her car that she released his hand.

"So?" she asked nervously awaiting being told what to do. Secretly she wished he would lean down and kiss her again, but on the lips this time.

She got her wish, Coach gave her, her first kiss. It was soft, sweet, and witnessed.

"Sho-nuff?" Margie exclaimed as she saw her co-worker kiss a student. 'No wonder he's running from me,' she thought.

She had been offering her services to Coach from the second he began working there. Not services actually, she wanted to fuck him.

She assumed that Teresa must be the reason he didn't take the bait. It wasn't. Margie looked like a shaved baboon wearing a horse costume that was the reason.

A wave of emotions swept through her body when his lips touched hers. The strange feeling overwhelmed Teresa causing her to flee.

"I have to go!" She whined and rushed into her car. She sped out of the parking lot and onto the freeway. Finally she slowed down at the sight of a police cruiser in front of her. A huge grin slowly spread on her face as she calmed down. She fondly recalled the feel of the stiff dick on her back.

A million conflicting thoughts battled for attention in her mind until she found herself pulling into her driveway.

"Hey daddy!" she beamed at her father, as he backed his car out of the large driveway. He smiled and waved back. He was heading out to handle the affairs of the church. Pun intended, she parked the car and skipped into the back door.

"Hey momma!" she sang planting a sideways kiss on her mother's pretty face.

"Hey yourself," Mary smiled, turned, then frowned. "Chile did you go out in those tight pants!"

After the close call Teresa decided to keep her distance from Coach. Every time theirs eyes met she quickly snatched her gaze away. The memory of his touch refused to die that easily. She was in agony every time she saw him.

Coach gave up after a couple of days and backed off. Once he caught her alone he finally spoke.

"Look, I'm sorry if I offended you. The kiss was out of line," He offered sounding sincere.

"Oh, don't be! You've done nothing wrong," Teresa replied. She meant to be stoic and blunt but got caught in his gaze. "It's just... I um... you know we can't...I need to see you again!"

"Come to my apartment!" Coach blurted out surprising even himself. He knew she was a minor, even though age of sexual consent is sixteen. Still with him being her teacher sex would be felonious.

"Let's both play hooky tomorrow," Teresa readily agreed. He almost said "No" and moved on with his life, but almost doesn't count, especially when it comes to statutory rape. It would be futile to say "well your honor I 'almost' didn't fuck her".

That night the junior pastor pulled out all the stops to prevent going through with the plans. He prayed, read his Bible, even spoke in tongues. Nothing worked to subdue his lustful desires. He couldn't even masturbate it away. And he tried that too.

In the end he decided to send her straight to school if she showed up at his apartment. That was until he pulled the door open the next morning. He took one look at her and ushered her inside.

Teresa rushed straight into his arms and kissed him. She had been up late contemplating the situation as well. The verdict was that her virginity was for her one day husband, but Coach could touch her if he wanted to. She may even touch him back. But that would be it, no intercourse.

Everything between entering the apartment and lying naked on Mathew's bed was a blur.

"Lawd! Lawd!" he exclaimed at the sight of her body.

"Lawd is right!" Teresa thought as he stripped down to his boxer briefs.

The junior pastor wasted no time in putting his face between her legs. He inhaled deeply, savoring the sweet smell of vagina. Nothing like it. He pulled her hairy lips open and licked her to an instant orgasm.

It was the most intense feeling she ever experienced in her short life, and just like clothes and phones, and purses and everything else, it became an addiction for her.

"Do it again!" she demanded once her body stopped quivering.

Coach quickly complied but this time positioned his body where she could touch him. Teresa took the bait and pulled his dick free. Dicks don't need instructions so she knew automatically to stroke it. She was amazed when it swelled even larger and expelled wads of semen. Shortly after getting him off she squealed from another orgasm.

The couple recuperated in silence, each caught up in their own emotions. The sexual floodgates had opened in both their lives. There would be no closing them. Coach knew it meant trouble but was powerless to stop himself.

Teresa was fascinated by her first sexual encounter. Not only did she replay it on her drive back home, but found herself watching porn on her computer once she got in. She watched all kinds of sex acts until she finally had to please herself. She was addicted to dick. It was only the start of an addictive personality that could ruin her and everyone around her.

Chapter 3

The sexual encounter awakened demons in the junior pastor he long subdued. The taste of Teresa's sweet virginal twat lingered on his tongue for days. He knew she was not ready for sex so he began to shy away from her.

It became increasingly hard to resist all temptations and flirtations. Eventually he gave in and fell into the same licentious behavior that sent him into the church in the first place.

"I see you only like young girls," Margie said confronting him in the empty teachers' lounge. "Oh I saw you! At the mall, you kissed that McCoy girl on the mouth."

"What do you want?" Mathew pleaded fearfully. He didn't doubt her since he was foolish enough to have met her openly.

"Same thing you gave her," Margie demanded looking at his crotch.

Coach frowned at the thought of eating the ape like woman's vagina, but the thought of sex sent blood rushing to his dick.

"This!" He asked freeing his erection. "This what you want?"

Margie couldn't answer with his dick in her mouth but he got the point. The fact that the unlocked door could swing open and cost both of them their jobs only heightened the act.

Coach snatched himself out of her mouth, one stroke short of climax, and bent the ugly woman over the sofa. He wanted to sample some gorilla pussy. And who could blame him.

"No wonder!" Mathew nodded as he stroked the moaning woman. He often wondered why apes had sex so often, cuz they got some good pussy.

"Turn around and drink!" He ordered as he pulled out. Margie quickly complied and allowed him to cum in her open mouth. It wasn't until he stopped skeeting that she saw him filming it with his phone.

"Freak!" she laughed as she licked the cum from her lips.

"Well, yeah, plus you want to blackmail me. I go down, you go down too," he laughed. Just then the pretty school nurse stuck her head in.

"Oh!" She exclaimed and quickly, shut the door.

"That bitch gonna say something!" Margie whined.

"Nah! She'll be alright," Coach said calmly. The nurse been flirting with him too. He planned on fucking her next, and did.

In a month he had bedded several teachers, the nurse, two lunch ladies, and the guidance counselor. In between he would watch the girls from his office window while masturbating. He was now wide open!

Teresa saw him standing in the window and decided to confront him about his ignoring her. When coach saw her marching towards his door he scrambled to put his dick away.

The lack of attention was something the spoiled girl could not endure. She accepted it at first but her hubris demanded she go check him.

"So you got what you wanted from me and kick me to the curb?" She asked with her hands on her full hips. Coach could clearly see the imprint of her vagina through the shorts, and his dick throbbed.

"That's not the case at all! I just think we, well I, went too far," He stammered.

"I say it didn't go far enough! I'm coming over in the morning, be ready!" She insisted and stormed off.

****

"You sure you're ready for this?" Mathew asked as he lubed the head of his swollen dick with her own juices.

"Y...Y...Yessss," she whimpered as he rubbed himself on her clit.

This wasn't the first cherry he popped so he knew exactly what to do. After easing halfway inside he gently stroked the tight box. Once he got her open a bit he plunged deep inside of her. Coach ignored her pleas to take it easy and fucked her savagely. Suddenly he pulled out and erupted on her stomach.

"Shit!" Mathew exclaimed, as he slumped over on top of her. Teresa let him lay there until he caught his breath before speaking.

"Do it again!" she demanded. They spent the rest of the school hours engaged in sex.

"Next Monday," Teresa said, setting her next appointment, as he led her to the front door.

"That's a date," Coach agreed with a slap on her firm ass. Unfortunately, Coach didn't make it until next week. He had done well restricting his dick to his middle age coworkers but that tight young pussy had turned him out. He could no longer turn down all the fast young girls.

He fucked one on Tuesday and two on Wednesday, and Thursday he was led away in handcuffs. If them little girls couldn't keep their legs closed, why did he think they would keep their mouths closed?

Junior Pastor Mathew Jenkins accepted a ten year sentence for child molestation, leaving Teresa to deal with her demons on her own. Porn and masturbation fed her thirst for sex but only for a while. Something had to give soon, and soon something did.

Chapter 4

"Teresa this is Michael, Michael my daughter Teresa," Mrs. McCoy beamed as she introduced the handsome new neighbor. "He moved in with Mrs. Graves to help her out."

Teresa thought her mom's giddiness was odd but let it pass. The woman was so prim and proper it was something seeing her this happy.

"Hey Teresa," Michael smiled extending his hand, "Mrs. Graves is my grandmother."

"Oh okay, nice to meet you," Teresa said forcing a smile to be polite. The second she touched his hand something stirred inside of her. It had been almost a year since Coach left.

"Where are you off to honey?" Teresa's mom said dismissing her. "Do you need money?"

"Sure, why not?" Teresa said accepting the bribe assuming it was meant to keep him away from her.

Michael however viewed the attractive young girl as just that, an attractive young girl. He had set his sights on her attractive mother. The flirting began so subtly neither of them realized at first. Teresa flirts got her nowhere, but frustrated. She was so unaccustomed to being ignored and she was fuming. To make matters worse, she saw the growing attraction between her mother and the neighbor.

Pastor McCoy was so busy in the church, Sister Clarice had begun to accompany him daily. Mrs. McCoy meanwhile relished in the new found attention even though she was drifting apart from her daughter.

Soon the relationship became strained and they began to bicker daily. Finally Teresa decided Michael was the root of the problem and should feel her wrath. She often watched him smoke weed in the backyard. So the next time she saw him alone she approached him. She marched right over, like the fussy brat that she was, and got in his face.

"I know what you're doing!" She exclaimed hotly.

"What?" Michael proclaimed innocently. "It's just a little reefer."

"With my mom! I know what you're doing!" She retreated. Michael was mortified that her daughter knew about the affair. They had only slept together the day before and wondered how they got found out so quickly. He shot a glance to the McCoy's driveway making sure the pastor's car wasn't there.

"I'm sorry, it just, just happened, I'm so sorry!" He pleaded.

That was when Teresa realized it was far worse than even she assumed. Never in her wildest dreams would she have assumed her mother was having sex with the man. Not the preacher's wife. She was mad at her mother for hogging the man's attention, but this would work in her favor.

"So that's why you won't look at me! Too busy fucking my mother!" She said loudly.

"Please, I'm sorry, please don't tell your father, he's been so nice to my grandma and me," Michael begged.

"And that's how you repay him? By fucking his wife!" She shot back. "I should tell him, but I won't. Of course you'll have to do something for me in return."

"Anything! Just name it," he sighed happy for a way out. "Whatever you want!"

****

"Oh yes! Right there!" Teresa shrieked as her neighbor found her clit with his tongue. He got into a rhythm and sucked her into a shuddering orgasm. Her price for silence was getting her pussy ate daily. She would sneak over once her dad left and mother was consumed with her own task. A few days later Michael was tongue fucking Teresa when they both heard her mother calling from downstairs.

"Michael?" She announced wickedly as she ascended the stairs. She entered the bedroom a split second after her daughter ducked naked into the closet. "We only have a few minutes, Pastor will be home any second."

Before Michael could stop her she dropped down and snatched his dick out of his shorts. He already had a rock hard erection from eating Teresa. He tried to protest but once he felt her hot mouth envelope his manhood he forgot. He even forgot about the girl in the closet as he stroked her face.

Teresa was amazed watching her prim and proper mother suck a dick. After a couple of minutes she got up and hiked her skirt over her hips.

"Fuck me!" she demanded on her hands and knees. Michael complied by shoving himself deep inside her. He pounded her so hard the sounds of their skin slapping together echoed in the otherwise quiet room.

"Whose pussy is this?" Michael inquired as he tapped her cervix.

"Mmm mmm," Mrs. McCoy said shaking her head vigorously.

"Tell me!" he demanded punctuating the query with long hard strokes. "I...said...whose...pussy...is...this?!"

Still the preacher's wife shook her head 'No'.

"Fine, I don't want it then!" he said, pulling himself out of her since she refused to name names.

"No please, please fuck me!" She pleaded causing Teresa to grimace. It only got worse when she crawled after the dick. When she caught it she swallowed it, only pausing to ask him to put it back in her.

"Please baby fuck me!" She begged shamelessly.

"Not until you tell me whose it is," Michael said laying on his back. "If it ain't mine I don't want it."

"It's yours baby," she conceded, "It's your pussy daddy."

Michael smiled and guided her on top of him. She grabbed his dick and wriggled it inside of her. Mrs. McCoy took a few slides up and down on his dick then grudged fucked him. She climaxed and kept right on riding.

"I'm coming!" Michael announced tapping her ass for her to get up. The married woman hopped off and rushed him back into her mouth. They both moaned loudly as he ejaculated.

"Mmm..I gotta go," Mary McCoy announced wiping away dribble of semen from her lips. She got up and pulled her skirt back down, leaving as quickly as she came.

Michael was shocked when Teresa busted angrily from the closet. She was upset for her father more than for herself and disgusted with her mother.

"I hate you!" She screamed in the man's face before racing down the stairs herself. She made it in the back door just in time to see her dad give his wife a warm kiss.

"What have you been eating?" The reverend asked smacking his lips trying to identify the taste.

Teresa fought the urge to tell him what it was. It took everything she had to refrain from telling her dear daddy he just tasted dick.

Chapter 5

Mrs. McCoy sought to appease her increasingly distant child by throwing money at her. It was the same technique her husband had been using on her lately. Sister Clarice got most of his time but she got the money.

"This doesn't make what you're doing okay you know," Teresa spat bitterly as she stuffed her mother's cash into her new designer purse. The recent influx of money fed into yet another addiction, the girl was a purse-a-holic as well as a shoe junkie.

"Why whatever do you mean dear?" She replied innocently, so innocently, Teresa might have went for it if she hadn't seen her fuck the man with her own eyes.

"Michael, you and Michael, I know what you're doing!" She repeated, "How could you do daddy that way!"

"Your father!" Mrs. McCoy yelled before catching herself. She took a deep breath to collect her thoughts before resuming.

"Daddy and I have a complex situation. It's not easy being a preacher's wife, having to share your husband on so many levels," she said in a calculated tone.

"Whatever" Teresa grunted and walked off. She headed up Cascade Road into another world.

The landscape changed dramatically as she entered the ghetto. She was picking up her classmate Leticia whom she had recently gotten close with. They had been in the same classes together since freshman year, but Teresa thought her crass and beneath her.

Now, she found her bold and exciting. That's just what she needed in her life, some excitement.

"Hey gurl," Leticia sang as she jumped into the passenger seat.

"Sup," Teresa replied taking in her skimpy outfits. She thought she was risqué with her close fitting jeans and tight little tee, but Leticia only had on some booty shorts and a wife beater.

"Look what Danté gave us," Leticia proclaimed producing a neatly rolled blunt.

"What is it?" Teresa asked with a smile since her friend's demeanor indicated it was something good.

"Chile please, I know you done smoked a blunt befoe!" She laughed.

"Smoked one! I ain't never even seen one be...um...foe," Teresa replied ebonically, as she tried to peek at it while she drove.

"Well you finna smoke one today!" Leticia said pushing in the cars never before used lighter.

"Are you serious?" She laughed nervously looking around for cops. Leticia put the glowing lighter to the cigar and inhale deeply. As the sweet aroma of the ATL's finest loud pack filled the car. Her mother's stern warnings about drugs rushed into her mind as Leticia passed the blunt to her.

"Hmp!" Teresa thought at the hypocritical advice. Mrs. McCoy had taken to smoking weed and drinking lately with her boyfriend so her admonishing was moot. Teresa took the weed with her free hand and gingerly took her first drag. She mimicked what her friend did holding the smoke in and taking sips of air.

"OKAAAAY!" Leticia cheered proudly. As if drug use and abuse were something to be proud of. By the time Teresa exhaled the smoke she had felted its mellowing effects.

"Wow," she said as the warm and fuzzy glow of its intoxication engulfed her.

"You know what? Let's hit the West End Mall, screw Lennox."

Leticia frowned at the suggestion. She grew up a stone's throw from the ghetto mall and had hoped to hit the more upscale Lennox Mall. There she had a chance to spot a real celebrity as opposed to the Trap Stars that frequented the West End.

Teresa was amazed at the wild ghetto kids. The boys all sported dreadlocks and gold grills. They wore baggy pants and shorts low off their butts exposing colorful boxer shorts. The girls too were ghetto fabulous as well, with extravagant hairstyles piled high on their heads. None of them wore much clothing. Teresa wondered how they got out of their homes wearing so little. She wore more clothing to bed than these girls wore out in public. She had no way of knowing that most of their young mothers were somewhere half naked as well.

Leticia seemed to know everybody and had to stop and greet someone else every few feet. All the girls begged her to tell Dante 'hey' while the boys made blunt come-ons.

One actually asked if he could fuck. Just like that, "Can I fuck?" and Leticia told him, "We'll see."

None of them paid Teresa any attention. She felt like Ms. Frumpy in her jeans & shirt. Still the hood mesmerized her and she wanted more of it. She went store to store buying the same cheap outfits the ghetto girls wore. She was amazed at how cheap everything was. The concept of buying one pair of shoes and getting a second pair free tickled her to no end.

One thing about the hood everyone dresses, talks, and acts the same. It amused her how loud everyone was. How they had conversations from across the store which was a 'no-no' in her universe. She even picked up a copy of the D-Lite album that everyone was going so crazy about and blasted on the way back to Leticia's house.

When she pulled into the driveway she got her first glimpse of Dante. He was shirtless and fabulous as he washed his motorcycle. His chiseled body was covered in crude prison tats and glistening from sweat. His shoulder left dreads were all over the place giving him a deliciously disheveled appearance.

"Oh my" Teresa replied still staring at the sweaty young man.

"Gurl stop!" Leticia laughed when she saw what had her friend so distracted. "Let me tell you 'rat now, my brother ain't shit! He got 'foe baby mamas and brang another hoe home err day!"

"I'm no hoe," Teresa replied inwardly, not at all swayed by the warn-ing. She always got what she wanted and now she wanted him. Danté saw Teresa staring and made his approach. He felt it was his duty to stick his dick in all his sister's friends.

"Sup y'all?" He asked leaning into the passengers' window.

"Un uh Danté! Go on now, she ain't like that," Leticia demanded.

Danté blew Teresa a kiss and that made her lonely vagina quiver. She could not help but admire the pretty thug with his ghetto swag. The question was not if she would sex him, only when. As she pulled out of the driveway she locked eyes with the beautiful man and made a tacit arrangement to fuck him first chance she got.

*****

That chance took a few months before it came around. In the mean-while she listened to Leticia relate her sexual encounters with several men. She felt a need to call and fill her in each time.

"Gurl Man-Man's dick was so thick!" She reported after her first date with Mr. 'Can I fuck' from the mall. She gave such vivid descrip-tions of the sex, Teresa found her finger making circles on her clit. For-tunately Leticia talked just for the sake of talking and missed the whim-per of her friend reaching an orgasm.

The situation in the McCoy household deteriorated by the day. Reverend McCoy was livid about coming home to a drunken wife sev-eral times. The handsome neighbor was introducing her to several of his drug habits along with his dick. Her husband could only identify the alcohol.

They usually got their child out of the house with a bribe so they could argue. She spent the money feeding her addictions of shopping and smoking weed. Now that it was her asking for the drug, Leticia made her pay then got it for free and pocketed the money. Teresa was high as a kite as she pulled into her driveway and saw her father sitting on the porch swing.

"We need to talk," he said stoically and slid over on the bench, "Have a seat."

'Oh my God! He knows I'm high' Her THC paranoia screamed.

"Sure daddy" she replied and sat down next to her. She leaned to the side to keep him from smelling the marijuana she just smoked. However, Reverend had bigger things on his mind.

"Well, may as well give it to you straight. Your momma is gone," he sighed.

'Where, next door?' Teresa mused, but said, "Gone where daddy?"

"She ran off with that young fella next door," he replied plainly. Oddly there wasn't a trace of sorrow over the loss of his wife of 20 years in his voice.

"Oh I'm so sorry daddy!" She wailed wrapping him in her arms. "That's fine daddy, we'll be just fine without her! Just the two of us, we'll make it!"

"Well," Rev paused, "Ya see, umm .... well it seems Sister Clarice and deacon Jones came to a parting ways too, so umm, well, sister gonna come stay here with us for a spell."

'Knew you was fucking that lady' Teresa laughed to herself. She thought she had seen a spark between them. Caught glances whispers.

"Ok, that's fine daddy," Teresa sang. She couldn't care less as long as it didn't slow up her own life. He could move the whole choir in for all she cared. "I still need my same allowance daddy."

"I believe your due a little raise, you're a good child, I couldn't ask for better," He said now returning the hug.

Over the next couple of weeks Teresa's weed smoking increased to every day. She and Danté played a flirtatious game of cat and mouse until she finally managed to catch him alone.

"Hey girl I'm almost there," Teresa advised upon taking Leticia's call.

"My bad shawty, I finna go with dis guy I just met at the gas station. He got a Benz," Leticia said excitedly.

"I can't believe you finna stand me up foe some dick!" Teresa exclaimed in flawless Ebonics. She was very proud of now being bi-lingual. "I needs me a sack of weed too!"

"Gurl Danté hur you can get it from him. I gotta go here come....umm...? Shit, that boy ain't even tell me his name!" Leticia said and hung up as a car horn sounded behind her.

The thought of seeing Danté alone involuntarily flexed Teresa's right leg causing her to press down on the gas pedal. Her tires actually chirped from turning onto their street too fast. When she pulled up to the house Danté was out front holding court with his fellow goons. Of course he was shirtless and gorgeous.

'Girl what are you doing?' Teresa chided herself as she approached the group of men. The reaction of his friends caused Danté to turn around.

"Who dat?" A gold grilled dread asked excitedly.

"One of my sister's friends. She ain't talking 'bout nothing' he replied turning his attention back to his guest. "She ain't here."

"I ain't here to see her," Teresa said so seductively, the whole earth got quiet.

"Sho-nuff?" Danté asked, turning back around to give her his full attention. "So what you doing? Huh? You tryna cut something?"

"I have no idea what that means," Teresa admitted with a giggle. "But I'm down for whatever."

"I'ma holla," he told his friends without even looking back. Danté led her to his motorcycle and helped her climb on behind him.

The vibrations of his bike combined with her arms wrapped around the sexy man threatened to make her cum. Danté whipped that bike through the light weekend traffic over to Moreland Ave. He pulled off the highway and into the parking lot of a rundown hotel.

Its sign read "Rooms by the hour" and skinny crack whores scurried about. Teresa frowned at the shabby place but didn't complain. She followed him into the office and watched as he paid the toothless clerk twenty dollars for The Room.

"We only got an hour," he explained as he led her into the dark room. The stench of stale beer, cigarette smoke, and body odor assaulted her nostrils but Danté seemed immune to it. He dropped his baggy shorts and climbed onto the bed.

"Come out dat shit shawty," He demanded nicely.

"Oh pardon me," Teresa apologized and began undressing as carefully and meticulously as she had gotten dressed hours before. She neatly folded her clothes, sat them on the table. "I must be eaten prior to intercourse," Teresa instructed as she joined him on the bed.

"Do what?" Danté exclaimed at the foreign words. "I don't eat no pussy shawty, but I'm finna hit it real good foe you."

"Oh my!" She gasped as he roughly threw her legs high in the air. He locked the back of her knees into the crook of his elbows and shoved himself inside her.

"Shit you got some wet-wet!" He marveled once he was safely inside of her, "And dis shit is tight!"

There was no tenderness as he slammed in and out of her. Teresa could only clench her teeth and take the rough sex. She loved it! So much that she didn't care that most of his tattoos were spelled wrong. Or that he was inside of her raw. A few minutes into the beating Danté plunged all the way in and climaxed inside of her.

Determined to get his twenty bucks worth he took a quick shower and jumped back inside of Teresa. Teresa was totally sprung, addicted.

*****

Despite Leticia's vehement objections, Teresa continued to date Danté. Perhaps date isn't the proper term. Whenever his drug dealing, baby mamma schedule allowed he would take her to a hotel and fuck her brains out. They never shared a meal, saw a movie or even held hands. Hell they never had an in depth conversation about anything.

Teresa did spend as much time trying to get a meal out of the man as he spent trying to talk his way into her mouth. Finally a deal was struck, she agreed to give him some head provided he take her out to eat. Even Leticia's multiple suitors had to feed her to fuck her, whether she knew their name or not.

"Man! This is not what I had in mind!" Teresa griped as he pulled his Donk into the drive thru of a hamburger joint.

"Shit shawty you ain't say what I had to feed you, just said feed you," Danté laughed.

"No deal! You can't get head from a kid's meal. Unless you plan on eating too," she said seductively.

Teresa frowned at the box Chevy that pulled up to the driver's side. It was parked down the block when they left his house and followed them. Danté was too busy ogling her thighs and she lacked the hood sense to register the danger.

It wasn't until one of the goons jumped out and began firing at the back of his head. Teresa screamed louder than the nine millimeter that destroyed Danté's skull. When the shooting stopped she was covered in blood and brain matter and had a lone dread lock still attached to the piece of skull in her lap.

The poor girl was in shock and had to be taken to an area hospital. Her troubled father arrived minutes after being notified. The reverend just could not figure how his daughter came to be at a murder scene. How she ended up in the car of a known felon, a drug dealer, a thief.

The harsh wake-up call had woke her up. Teresa wanted nothing to do with anything even remotely ghetto. That included Leticia as well. It took a week of cold shoulders and unreturned calls and text before she got the message.

For the rest of her senior year, her focus was on school and church. She had enough. Lesson learned.

Chapter 6

As expected Teresa was accepted into every college she applied for. Seeking to distance herself from herself she selected a private Christian college in Alabama.

Reverend McCoy and Sister Clarice drove down behind her to help her get situated in her dorm. She and Clarice had gotten quite close in her mother's absence.

"This is nice," Clarice said as they entered the small room. He sat down the huge suitcase and went to retrieve the rest of her belongings.

"Let's go look around campus and grab lunch," Teresa's dad suggested.

"Come on Rev, let's let her get settled in. We'll come down in a couple of weeks and she can show us around," Sister Clarice insisted. She didn't want to cramp her style by dragging her parents around.

"Well, okay I guess," he relented then turned to his daughter. "Since this is a Christian school I guess I won't have to worry about boys or drugs or alcohol, or ...."

"Daddy!" Teresa whined, "I'll be fine."

Again the pastor naively assumed that these kids were different than any others. In some regards they were even worse. As soon as her parents left, her roommate arrived with hers.

Leslie was a very pretty and very dark girl with a killer body and zero self-esteem.

"God bless you, I love you," the sweet girl proclaimed with a hug as an introduction. Her mother greeted her the same way while her stoic father looked on from the hallway. Leslie's fussy mother stayed and helped her daughter unpacked and put her belongings away. She even instructed her which drawers to put what in. Her father led them in a fifteen minute prayer before they finally left.

That night a so-called "meet and greet" was held. What it really was, was a full fledge party and it was off the hook!

The repressed preachers' kids had finally had a chance to breathe and breathe they did! Later that night the sound of cherries being popped could be heard for miles.

Teresa and Leslie both wore tasteful ankle length sundresses. Both were grossly over-dressed. Most of the females rushed to the local mall and bought their real college clothes the second their parents left.

"Oh my God!" Leslie exclaimed at the sight of hundreds of half-naked kids. The girls wore tiny skirts or shorts and showed cleavage. The guys were in wife beaters and a few were shirtless.

The Devil's music was blasted from the D.J. booth and the make shift dance floor was full of the kids dry humping each other. Guys flocked to the two pretty freshmen as soon as they stepped into the room.

They were "New Meat" and the race was on to fuck them first. Teresa having had a taste of the real world handled the attention like a vet. She was all, "thank you but no" rejecting all advances.

Leslie on the other hand was terrified. She had been homeschooled her whole life by her overzealous parents. If they could have taught her college courses, they would have done that too. She actually cowered in fear behind Teresa whenever a guy approached.

"Calm down Leslie. Just smile and say, no thank you," Teresa encouraged.

As the night drew on she came out of her shell a little and carried on conversations with a few guys.

"He was cute," Teresa said of one guy Leslie was speaking to.

"Yeah! And nice too. He asked me to come to his room so he can show me his videos!" she gushed naively.

"Chile he wants to make a video!" Teresa warned.

"I don't understand?" Leslie frowned.

"Girl he wants to fuck you on camera and show all his friends!" she spelled out.

Leslie was so repulsed at the notion she crossed her arms and covered herself. When he returned with his glass of spiked punch she threw it in his face.

"How dare you! We're not married!" she yelled confusing the film major. He really did want to show her the documentary he just made, and was very proud of.

Once word of her virginity spread, her cherry would be sought after like the Holy Grail. This school like every school had virgin hunters. Cherry poppers, Hymen-He-men! It didn't matter if a girl was tall, short, pretty, ugly, fat or skinny. If her hymen was intact they were coming for it.

*****

As the school year wore on eventually both girls became more receptive to male company. They were the only girls not going out to dinner, or movies. Both harmless past times, totally innocuous right? Yeah right.

"Ladies," a handsome junior, by the name of Darrin Sanders, greeted showing off his brilliant smile.

Although the word was plural he only looked at Teresa. They had been playing eye-tag for weeks but this was the first time they had a chance to speak.

"I'm Darrin and this is my buddy Edwin." He said looking into Teresa's being.

"Hey Darrin, I'm Teresa and this is my friend...umm.... Leslie," she replied having to actually look at her roommate to recall her name. Edwin and Leslie began to chat it up separately when Teresa and Darrin strolled off. On their walk around campus Darrin explain his presence in her life. He too was from Atlanta, but one of its more affluent surrounding counties. His father was a part time minister and full-time chairman of a utility company. That meant he was not only handsome, religious, funny, and smart, he was rich.

Teresa gave meaningless details of her life as well. Needless, because Darrin had already checked into her. He knew full well her father was a well-respected minister, who turned down the helm of a mega-church and the riches that went along with it. He was royalty among Atlanta clergy. She was his ticket into the inner circle.

Edwin was making an impact on Leslie's life as well, however it was in a different direction. He knew she was one of the few remaining virgins on campus. The only one under two hundred and fifty pounds; the bounty on her cherry was highly sought after. It actually had a wanted poster.

"Let's get some punch," Edwin suggested leading her to the punch bowl. The fruity punch was highly sweetened to mask the massive amount of 190 proof liquor.

"Mmm this is good," Leslie said politely.

It wasn't, but she did want to please her new friend. She spent her entire young life watching her mother dote over her father and being treated like a queen in return. That's why she drank the next two cups he offered. She could be his queen.

"Let's go out and walk," Edwin suggested eager to get her somewhere alone. Her virgin system had already been altered by the alcohol as she slurred her approval. She was pissy drunk by the time they left. Edwin barely got her back to the room before she completely passed out. No matter, he didn't mind. At least this way she would be open for anything he suggested.

"Dayum!" He marveled at how fine her dark body was as he stripped her naked. For the next hour Edwin date raped the unconscious girl. He propped her helpless body in a variety of positions and had his way with her.

Being the savage that he was he neither wore a condom or pulled out. Instead he ejaculated in her several times. He wished he had more time with her but knew her roommate would return at any second. Again he cursed his decision not to take her to his room. There, he would have had more time. There he had a video camera. He had no problems selling footage of himself having sex with unconscious women. There's actually a market for that sort of thing.

"Edwin?" Teresa asked curiously when she ran into the rapist on the stairs. "Where's Leslie?"

"She... Uhh...." He mumbled something incoherently, and rushed past her and out of the building.

His presence and demeanor alerted Teresa and she made a dash to her room.

Why is he even here, she wondered taking the steps by twos. She and Darrin had a wonderful walk and talk, and he didn't so much as touch her hand.

"Oh No!" She wailed as she entered her dorm room. There was Leslie completely naked on her bed. Her legs were still spread wide like Edwin had left her. When Teresa approached she saw blood tinged semen leaking out of her.

"Leslie? Leslie!" Teresa demanded attempting to wake her friend. When the girl would not stir she knew whatever happened was not consensual. Her friend had been raped.

Not knowing exactly what she should do Teresa filled a container with warm soapy water and washed her friend. She remembered Leticia's claims that a douche after unprotected sex will prevent pregnancy. She used two of them on her friend. She was spring fresh now but would that be enough?

The next morning Leslie woke up disoriented and confused. Her head hurt just as much as her sore vagina but neither made sense. Since she had no memory of the incident Teresa decided not to tell her. She didn't need to know. The hell she didn't!

Chapter 7

Over the next few months Darrin and Teresa had become inseparable. Whenever they couldn't be in each other's company they filled the void with text messages and emails.

Darrin was deeply religious, so Teresa decided she was too. No matter how horny she got she never made a move. She was a good girl just like he wanted. She even cut off all her porn and masturbation as she really began to change.

He had made it clear that he wanted to marry her but that his future wife must be a virgin. Teresa was delighted even though she hadn't figured out how she was going to pull off the virgin part.

Edwin on the other hand had never came around again after. He had conquered 'Mount Hymen' and was off in search for more prey. The snub deeply affected the girl who already suffered from an unhealthy dose of low self-esteem, sinking her lower into an abyss.

She retreated into her Bible and long bouts of prayer; until finally, a miracle happened.

"Teresa sit down I have amazing news!" Leslie gushed bouncing up and down.

"What you deciphered the book of numbers?" Teresa joked. She was happy already finally seeing some joy in the girl.

"I deciphered numbers years ago. This is bigger, way bigger! A miracle! The second coming and he chose me. ME!" She yelled on the verge of hysteria.

"Girl what are you talking about?" Teresa laughed amused.

"I know you're going to find this hard to believe. I hardly believe it myself. I have never been with a man, but I'm with child!"

"Excuse me, you what!" Teresa asked becoming alarmed.

"I haven't had my period in months. So last month on a whim I took a pregnancy test and it was positive. I didn't believe it so I took another one just now, and look!" Leslie exclaimed thrusting a positive dip stick at her.

She then lifted her shirt showing her slightly rounded belly.

That's not God's baby it's the Devil's Teresa fumed internally remembering Edwin sneaking off after raping her.

"Have you been to a doctor? You need to see a doctor." she asked urgently.

She now regretted her decision of not telling her what happened. The poor girl now thinks she's the virgin mother.

"We're fine, it's a special child. No harm can come to us." Leslie assured her.

"Child please! Come on!" She insisted practically dragging her stubborn roommate to her car.

Leslie relented but protested the whole way to the clinic. In the end Teresa convinced her that even if it was a miracle baby it was still human and needed medical care. They both exhaled a sigh of relief when a female doctor entered the examination room. Since so many girls from the school got pregnant every year they recruited mainly female M.D's.

"Okay...a pregnant virgin huh? Let's have a look," the doctor said without the slightest trace of sarcasm. This wasn't the first pregnant virgin to come from the Christian school. Every year she treats pregnancies and STD's of girls who *"never done it before!"*

A quick examination revealed her hymen had been ruptured, which itself doesn't always amount to sexual intercourse, but coupled with pregnancy there was no doubt.

"Two things," the doctor began as she slid her chair from between Leslie's open legs and removed her latex gloves. "You are definitely pregnant and you are not a virgin."

"Oh ye of little faith!" Leslie chided. She berated the "heathen" doctor while she dressed. Teresa overwhelmed by what she knew began to weep.

"We need to talk," Teresa said sadly as they rode back to campus. "There is something I need to tell you."

And tell she did. Leslie was eerily calm as Teresa informed her of being plied with alcohol and raped. She refused the offer of going to the police or campus security. Instead she begged for some time alone to think things through.

Teresa reluctantly relented and left her alone. She sat in the library and read the long awaited DOPE GIRL novel to escape the grim reality of the present. Darrin picked her up and took her for a bite to eat before taking her home. She was subdued with grief for her friend.

"What's wrong?" Darrin inquired after watching her toy with her food.

"Hmm? Oh, I'm sorry. Lots on my mind," she replied offering a weak smile.

Darrin was more concerned with the events in his life so he didn't pry further. When Teresa returned to the dorm room, Leslie was laying still under her covers. She knew then but denial talked her into bed.

The next morning she went to take an exam then returned to the dorm and called campus police to report the suicide.

Chapter 8

The college offered to automatically pass Teresa in all of her courses, as well as free grief counseling, she flatly refused both. She was far too angry for grief. She was hot and wanted revenge.

One of the girls in the dorms was generous enough to give her a pretty little pink pill to chase all the pain away. It was proof again that drugs could be useful. They can make one feel better. Now all that was left was the anger.

In her fury a plan was hatched. She purchased a surprisingly easy to obtain vile of GHB and spun her web. All she needed now was the insect. The particular insect proved elusive so Teresa staked out his dorm. It took a couple of days but she finally tracked him down.

"Oh hey Edwin!" She exclaimed happily when she *accidentally* ran into him.

"Hey um.. T, I gotta umm..." He stammered in an attempt to flee.

"Chill baby, why you keep avoiding me?" She whined seductively. "I'm trying to get with you."

The pussy hound heard the yearning in her voice and stopped in his tracks.

"So what you talking about then? And ain't you fucking with my boy D?" He asked licking her breast with his eyes.

"Ain't no fucking!" She replied wistfully. It appeared genuine, because it was. "I mean we still kick it but he ain't trying to fuck. You ever seen a man don't want no pussy? And I got that good wet-wet."

She knew full well that her plan, if it went well, could cost her Darrin's love but it was a risk she had to take. Sometimes revenge is more important than right and wrong.

"That nigga trippin! I'd fuck the shit out of yo fine ass!" Edwin announced. "I'm talking, from the back, side, all up in you!"

"For real! You would do it to me?" she asked as if honored. As if she won a prize in dick sweepstakes or something.

"Yeah, I'm saying though, I wouldn't mind hitting that for you but umm..." He said trying her up. Word around campus was that she had a little cake so why not get a slice to go along with that pie.

"But what?" She asked desperately. She was already fuming but when his reply came she almost lost her mind.

"You know I usually charge a bitch like... five hundred to break her in, but since you fuck with my boy just gimme two," he said smiling at the discount.

"Okay!" Teresa cheered, "Come through, say ten?"

"Ten it is," he nodded coolly, like a pimp.

******

"I'm here" Edwin texted to announce his arrival at Teresa's dorm.

"Cum on up" she replied.

Her research said she had approximately thirty minutes before the date rape drug rendered her incapacitated. She had to move fast.

She dropped the desired amount into her drink and tossed it back. The clock was ticking.

"Sup T, I... Shit!" Edwin exclaimed as he entered and saw what Teresa was wearing.

"You like?" She giggled doing a 360 so he could see her caramel ass cheeks protruding out of the black thong. Her firm breasts were hanging out of the matching bra.

"Do I!" He replied and moved on her. He wrapped her into his arms and led her backwards to the bed.

"Hurry!" Teresa pleaded as she scrambled for his zipper.

Edwin helped out and dropped his pants causing his erection to spring out and quiver up and down like a diving board.

Teresa was oddly turned on despite her plans. The fact of the matter was Edwin was fine and was armed with a big, solid dick.

"Get that shit off!" He demanded as he stripped.

"No, you take it off" she teased. "You want this pussy, you gonna have to take it."

"Oh you like it rough huh?" Edwin laughed standing over her.

"Mmm hmm. Rip it off. Take this pussy!" A rapist at heart had no problem tearing her panties in two. He snatched at the bra sending the clasps flying across the room.

"Shit you wet!" He marveled as he fondled her vagina.

"Fuck me Eddie, do it, do it hard!" She begged. She meant it too. Sure it was part of her plan, but why not get a nut out the deal?

He complied by roughly shoving himself inside of her. Mentally he patted himself on the back at yet another conquest. Teresa fought not to enjoy it but Edwin had a mean stroke. Before she could stop it, her body began to quiver as she came. He was right behind her and grunted loudly filling her with semen.

"Mmm," he moaned with pleasure. "Shit you got some good ass pussy!"

"You got some good ass dick," Teresa moaned caressing his shaft with her vagina muscles.

"Man I should have sucked it," she said haltingly as the drug began to take effect.

"Shit you still can!" He yelled pulling out of her vagina and into her face in a split second.

"Go wash it off first. It's all wet!" She frowned pushing it away. Edwin was so thirsty for some head he rushed out into the hallway completely naked. He ran down the hallway of the female only dorm with his dick bobbing in the air. He almost made it without being seen. Only one girl caught a glimpse of the naked man and quickly called campus security.

She wasn't the only one calling the police. As soon as he left the room Teresa swallowed the "morning after pill" and grabbed the phone.

"Campus security, how can I help you?" The monotone operator inquired.

"I, I ju.... just got raped, please he..." was all she got out before passing out.

"Babe?" Edwin said trying to rouse the girl when he returned with
a clean dick. When he couldn't wake her he shrugged his shoulders and
slid into her mouth anyway.

That's just how police found him when they rushed into the room.
How the fuck can you explain your dick in an unconscious girl's
mouth? The ripped underwear, the vaginal tears from rough sex, the
vagina full of your semen. The date rape drug in her system. You don't
that's how!

This was going to cost him 20 years of his life. Pay back is a bitch!

Chapter 9

Darrin was the first visitor received at the hospital. She was so shamed by the "rape" she couldn't even look at him. He too was deeply troubled and conflicted by the whole situation.

He grew up with Edwin, knew him his whole life. Yeah he was morally challenged but rape! On the other hand the police laid out the strong facts. Darrin sat down by her side and took her hand in his. He didn't speak though, at least not to her. Instead he prayed.

That's how Reverend McCoy found her when he rushed into the room an hour later.

"Baby!" He sighed with tears streaming down his face. He too had spoken with the police and knew all the sordid details. His precious daughter's virginity had been stolen.

"I'm ok daddy," Teresa whined and broke down as he scooped her into his arms. Darrin still didn't relinquish her hand which got daddy's full attention.

"Who are you young man!" He boomed down at him.

"I'm Darrin Sanders!" He replied proudly as he rose to his feet. He was honored to meet the clergy legend. He finally withdrew his hand from Teresa's and thrust it towards her father.

"Sir, I intend to marry your daughter. That's if she'll have me?" He added looking at her.

"Of course! Of course, I'll marry you!" Teresa screamed excitedly.

This was a win/win/win situation for her. Not only did her man propose but she now had an excuse about not being a virgin. To top it off the doctors gave her a supply of pills that made her feel good!

The sex, consensual or not, along with the drug, prescription or not, poked a hole in the dam of self-restraint? The effects were not immediate, but a flood was coming.

****

39

A few weeks after "the incident" Teresa had Darrin alone in her room, and she was all over him. The pain pill she was still taking had her humming and he smelt wonderful!

"Teresa! What's gotten into you!" He exclaimed shoving her hand away from his crotch.

"Baaabeeeeey! Please! Just a little affection?" She whined. "We're about to be married anyway."

It was his fault anyway coming over there in a tank top and shorts showing off his tall muscular frame. If not for being severely uncoordinated, he could have been a star athlete with a body like that.

"Well we're not married yet!" He said rising to his feet, "You need to take a cold shower, the flesh is weak!" He added as he rushed to the door on his way to do the same. His flesh wasn't weak it was hard.

Teresa was fuming. She was far too spoiled to have him or anyone tell her what she could or could not have. She began to touch herself but that did little to quench her thirst. Even after massaging herself to an orgasm she felt unfulfilled. She now wanted, no, needed to be filled up.

Every city and town has an underbelly, a "dark-side" a "cross the tracks" or "down bottom" where the black folks stay. This little Alabama town was no different. That's exactly where Teresa found herself heading. She located the small hole in the wall club and strolled in.

As she looked around the primitive establishment she stifled a chuckle. The place was straight out of "The Color Purple." She half expected Tweet to run up and declare, "this here our juke joint."

All eyes were on the obviously out of place stranger. The local women frowned at the woman who was a full light year out of their league, as all the men grinned feeling the same. They would be content with staring at the beautiful girl and talking about her for months to come.

Not Horace though, he had been out into the real world before. Since he was active duty military, he had been all over the world. He expected his weeklong leave to visit family and friends to be boring, until she walked in.

"You must be looking for me?" Horace smiled as he approached on muscular bowed legs. Plus he was fine! A nice solid 6'4 country boy. He was just what she was looking for.

"Must I?" Teresa shot back, impressed with his confidence. "And why is that?"

"Cuz caint not nare none of dese country boyz handle you," he joked in a mock drawl indigenous of the locals.

"And you think you can?" She demanded.

"I can show you better than I can tell you" he offered.

He turned and walked towards the door knowing she would follow him. She did. He led her to his car and opened the door for her. After closing it he came around and got in and pulled from the Juke Joint parking lot.

Teresa wondered what romantic spot he would chose for their romp. He swung a quick right causing her to frown.

"A corn field! Really?" She shook her head.

"Think of it as a five star cornfield and come on," he ordered and parked. "Besides, once I get this log inside you it won't matter anymore!"

Once outside of the car he picked Teresa up and placed her on the hood of the car. They locked eyes as he hiked her skirt up and began to fondle her vagina. She was so backed up she immediately soaked his fingers then came on them a second later.

"I could have done that myself," she quipped after climaxing. She left out the fact that she had.

"Well I reckon you don't have one of these." He bragged as he produced a well above average sized erection."

"I do now," Teresa laughed as she grabbed it and guided him inside of her.

"May I?" He asked politely as he pushed past her swollen outer lips.

"By all means," she moaned graciously accepting his generous offer.

Horace may have possessed the sweet manners of a southern gentlemen but he fucked like a roughneck. Teresa almost called him Danté when he pounded her to the first of what would be many orgasms.

She was spent by the time they left that cornfield but it didn't keep her from returning the next night. The night after either. For the entire week Horace was on leave he sexed the sex starved coed.

Teresa was Darrin's good girl by day and Horace's slut by night. She literally cried when time came for him to go back to the army. Almost asked to go with him. She would fight, she didn't mind, just don't take the dick away. Please!

The supply of medication kept her on an even keel but did nothing for Teresa's physical cravings. Darrin rejected her so forcefully that she gave up on getting anything out of him. She wisely refused to shit where she ate and didn't mess around on campus.

Word about who fucked who spread so quickly it was beyond belief. Sometimes before the deed was finished, sometimes before it even happened. You know black folk, they see you talking and *they fuckin'*.

Trips down bottom turned into sexual forays. At least once a week she made the short journey to get her rocks off. The local country boys couldn't believe it when they got selected for a foray into the corn field.

She began to master the art of hiding in plain sight. Teresa was one way around her father and fiancée, and quite another when alone. She refused to deny herself what she wanted.

Chapter 10

Even after Darrin graduated and returned to Atlanta, Teresa managed to juggle both worlds. She went home every weekend to keep the wolves away from her future husband. Darrin, now Reverend Sanders took the reins of his father's church. Reverend McCoy may have been his mentor but he still made plans to grow his congregation. He would not turn down the riches and more importantly fame that came along with a mega-church.

Two years later the couple tied the knot in an elaborate affair proceeding over by Darrin Sr. while Reverend McCoy proudly gave his daughter in marriage. Darrin Sanders Sr. was a gifted speaker and put on for the occasion.

All Teresa heard was 'blah, blah, blah'. She was ready to get on with it. She had been good for the last year and was ready to fuck something! The reception, carriage ride, cake cutting was all a blur. She was on auto-pilot during the short charter flight to Savannah. Life restarted for Teresa once they stepped into the honey moon suite of the coastal resort.

"Mmm Mr. Sanders! Teresa moaned as she pressed her body into her husbands. She smiled broadly feeling what had to be a pretty good sized dick pressing against her.

"Mmm yourself Mrs. Sanders," he moaned as the blood rushed from his brain to his dick.

"Ohh look! Champagne! She announced and went for the bucket.

"Babe you know we should not. You know what the Bible says about..."

"It is our honey moon. Special occasion, Loosen up," Teresa said filling two glasses. "To us!" She cheered clinking his flute with hers.

Darrin frowned from the bitter taste of his first drink, as Teresa drained her glass. She quickly re-filled and re-emptied her glass again. The couple made congenial small talk as she drank most of the bottle.

"Well shouldn't we um...?" Darrin asked pointing to the bed with his head.

"Thought you would never ask!" Teresa exclaimed. She slammed back the contents of the flute and walked over to the bed.

They stood on opposite sides of the bed and began removing their clothes. Darrin smiled brightly at the sight of his wife's stunning figure. Teresa too was pleased when his rather large dick came into view.

Teresa fought the urge to pump her fist and yelled, "YESSSS!" at the sight of his manhood. Having never seen it before she allowed herself to entertain the 'what if' he had a mini-man.

Since this was supposed to be minus the "rape" her first time having sex she pretended to be naive and demure. But since it really was his first time she had to take the lead.

"Slow and easy" she instructed as they began to kiss passionately.

"Oh my!" He reeled at the feel of her tongue when it slipped inside of his mouth.

"What's wrong baby?" She asked at the odd reaction.

"Your tongue" he chuckled, "It accidentally went inside of my mouth!"

Teresa shook her head and held her tongue, literally. She pulled his ample manhood and rubbed it on her eager vagina.

"It's so wet!" He giggled boyishly.

"Push baby" she begged after wriggling the head inside of her.

"Oh, my, goodness!" Darrin exclaimed one word per pump. Then slumped over on top of her, fighting for air.

"You did not just cum?" She practically yelled. "Tell me you did not just cum!"

"Yes Lawd," he affirmed, rolling onto his back gasping for air.

Teresa sat there for a second letting all profanities pass through her mind before she spoke. She took too long because her husband took a deep breath that exhaled as a snore. Dude was sleep!

"Can't believe this shit!" She whined as she began to masturbate. "Jackin off on my own damn wedding night!"

After getting herself off she got up and knocked off the rest of the champagne. That night pretty much set the tone of the couple's love life. He lasted a little longer the next night but sexually Teresa was on her own.

Ole Rev. could preach for hours on the pulpit but was next to useless in the pussy. He could hoop and holla for the congregation but could only last a couple minutes in his deprived wife. She realized early on that if she wanted satisfaction she would have to do it herself.

****

Darrin's main focus was the church. He intended to grow the church by any means. In a year he doubled the congregation and plans were made on a new complex. With her husband spending all his time and energy in the church Teresa needed something to occupy her idle time.

The urge for drugs and or some good sex were growing. Something had to be done, and soon. In an attempt to fight the urges off she decided to enter the work force. Her credentials allowed her to secure a teaching position.

All the local schools were fully staffed but there was oddly a wealth of empty slots in the inner city schools. Wondering why?

Not knowing any better Teresa took a job in one of the deprived inner city high schools. It was a harsh wake up call to real life. Teresa was amazed at how mature and hardened the ghetto kids were. Here she was a fully grown, fully married woman with no kids but has students with one, two, and three children already.

This is where she met M.J. His full name was actually Michael Jackson, but he would beat you up if you called him that. Even teachers and staff called him M.J. to be on the safe side.

The man-child was a year older than the rest of the senior class due to the year he took off for pre-trial incarceration on drug charges. Part of the plea deal that kept him out of prison was to stay in high school.

"Mari-Juwanna Jackson?" Teresa called struggling to get through her first roll-call. None of the kids had normal names. There were no David's or Mary's. Just Octdontavious and Shakwa-Nisha'a and of course Mari-Juwanna's.

It was as if the ghetto had called some secret contest for the hardest to pronounce name. Or perhaps welfare had to begin paying by the syllable. Most of those poor kids couldn't pronounce their own names until they were five and six years old.

"Hure!" Mari-Juwanna called out sticking up her hand embellished in gawdy tips. She whipped the green wig out of her blue contacts and resumed popping her gum.

"Michael Jackson!" Teresa summoned with ease.

Besides him, Carla Towns and Sandy Peoples, the entire class had tongue twisters for names. The sound of his full name started a small uproar in the over-crowded class.

"Uh-hu you ain't 'posed to call him dat," one girl barely managed to get out even though English was her first language.

"You gotta call him M.J.!" another warned.

"Alright, M.J.!" Teresa called.

M.J. stuck his long muscular arm up as the pretty ghetto girl next to him called "hure."

"Mrs... ummm, let's see here....Anna-costa-ria? Can M.J. speak for himself?"

"My name.... is Anna-Costa-Maria" she corrected moving her head sarcastically to punctuate each syllable.

"Well excuse me," Teresa said contritely, "But it's there a reason you're speaking for M.J.?"

"Cuz he my baby-daddy" she shot back as if everyone knew that and as if that explained it.

"Well Mr. M.J." She began as she walked to the rear of the class where he was seated. When she laid eyes on the student she forgot what she was saying.

M.J. sported a freshly cut head full of waves. His full beard was trimmed around his handsome face, perfectly. Of course, he wore all the latest fashions and was blinging quite nicely.

"Sup shawty? Stuck ain't ya," He chuckled causing the room to erupt with laughter.

M.J. exuded sexuality and when he ran his dark eyes over her body, she felt a tingle in every spot they touched.

"Say present, or here when your name is called!" She demanded regaining her composure.

"That's what's up" he nodded knowingly. M.J. was no stranger to the attractions of older women. He had already bedded several women including his probation officer. Even a few of his mother's friends and from the looks of it soon a teacher.

Teresa was delighted to see Darrin's car in the driveway. She planned to relieve her burning desire by laying under the faucet and letting the gentle stream of water get her off. But since her husband was home he would have to do.

Maybe, just maybe she could squeeze a nut out of the man. She was so turned on by her student she attacked her husband right on the sofa. Under protest she snatched his penis out of his slacks, grinding on it till it stood up on its own.

"What's gotten into you?" The surprised Reverend asked his wife as she eased down onto his dick.

"Mmm, been thinking about this all day," she replied. It was half true cause she did daydream about riding a dick, just not his.

She concentrated all her energy on the friction on her clit and felt the sensation slowly build.

'Finally gonna get me a nut out this man' she thought as she drew ever closer to the first orgasm of her marriage. Besides the self-inflicted ones that is.

"Mmm baby you about to make me ...." was all she got out before her husband spasmed beneath her.

"Alright!!!" he grunted as he climaxed and pushed her off of him.

"What the fuck is wrong with you!" Teresa demanded as she hit the floor.

"Awe shucks! Look at my slacks," he griped, ignoring his wife's complaint and needs.

Darrin was more concerned about the semen on his suite than the desperation of his wife. What happened next was his fault.

Chapter 11

"M.J!" Teresa called out yet a third time. Over the few weeks that school had been in session she had at least gotten him to cooperate with roll call if nothing else.

"He ain't in hur!" A severely literacy challenged girl replied. Poor child struggled with everything except what came on the radio. Maybe someone could rap about algebra or history.

She frowned knowing she had seen his truck in the student parking lot. He knew his being in class everyday was a condition of his probation. His continued freedom depended upon it.

He wasn't even required to pass, just show up. A glance around the room proved that he nor his seven syllable baby mama were in attendance. Teresa looked out her window and sure enough the custom S.U.V was there. It confused her for a second until she saw a hand extend from the driver's window and flick ashes of a blunt.

"La-la-da...um..La qua..um...you!" Teresa called the runner up for most difficult names. "Read chapter three until I return!"

That translated to "y'all lose y'all damn minds until I come back" as she marched out of the class.

As she approached the vehicle she could smell the aroma of potent marijuana that awakened a strong desire. The latest banger by Erv-G was rumbling his truck even at a low volume. Teresa took a deep breath, and prepared to read M.J. the riot act, until she looked into the truck. There was M.J. leaned back and Annacostamaria with a good portion of his dick in her mouth.

"Hey Mrs. Sanders," M.J. smiled with smoke billowing from his nostrils. Annacostamaria looked up and waved with her free hand. Teresa was too shocked to speak. She could only watch as the young girl worked his dick flawlessly with her hand and mouth.

M.J. laid his head back and closed his eyes. Occasionally she pulled it out her mouth and vigorously worked its thick shaft with her hand while planting kisses on its big head.

"I'm finna cum," M.J. announced causing baby mama to urgently get him back inside her mouth.

M.J. Stuck his hand out the window for his teacher and for reasons she could not explain she took it. He squeezed his teachers hand while holding Annacostamaria's head in place with the other. They moaned together as M.J. climaxed on her tonsils. Teresa felt her expensive panties become soaked at the display.

"Hey Mrs. Sanders 'scuse me for not speaking befoe', but he don't like me to talk while I give head." Annacostamaria smiled with a dribble of semen on the corner of her mouth.

"That's quite alright. I want you to go back to class while I speak with M.J.," Teresa instructed. "Oh and rinse your mouth out first."

"Okaay," the eager to please girl said, and scurried off towards the building.

"Part of your probation is that you attend class!" Teresa said to his deflating penis. M.J. tucked his dick away forcing eye contact.

"Chill Mrs. T," M.J. smiled dumbfounded as to how playing hooky to get head was related to her. "Shit a nigga dick be all hard looking at you in class! I couldn't take that shit no mo'!"

"Be that as it may!" Teresa said fighting a flattered smile, "I need you in my class!"

"Lady you need me in you," M.J. cut to the chase. "I'm finna go. Here."

"And what am I supposed to do with this?" she inquired about the half smoked blunt he placed in her hand.

"Smoke dat shit and chill the fuck out," M.J. instructed turning the ignition. "Check I'ma be rat here on Saturday, 3 o'clock."

"Well I won't!" she yelled after his truck as it left the parking lot. "You'll be here by yourself!"

****

"Girl what are you doing here!" Teresa asked herself again as she sat in the school's empty parking lot. It was now 3:30 and she was beginning to feel foolish.

"Plan-B" she sighed thinking of a rather large dildo she saw at the local head shop. She had stopped just short of buying it and came here instead. Teresa was on the verge of tears as she started her car. Here she was naked under her sundress waiting on a student to do what she absolutely could not get her husband. Just as she put her car in gear the boom of D-Lite's latest jam shook her mirrors. Seconds later M.J's truck appeared and pulled next to her.

"Do you know how to tell time?" Teresa demanded.

"Follow me shawty" he said and pulled off.

Teresa followed him eagerly, dipping in and out of traffic to keep up. Either he was an extremely reckless driver or he intended to make her work for the dick. In truth it was both. And work she did. By the time they reached the chain motel in the suburbs just north of Atlanta she was actually winded. They pulled into adjacent parking spaces and got out. M.J. bypassed the office and led her straight to an upstairs room.

"Dis my lil hide-out," he announced, using the key card to open the door.

"Quaint," she quipped stepping past him and entering the room. Her eyes surveyed the room before settling on a pile of white powder on the table. She curiously walked over to inspect it.

"Don't mind that, I was in the middle of bagging up when I 'membered you." He explained.

"What is it?" She asked feeling mesmerized by the glistening pile of powder.

"New Yawks finest! Skrate fish scale!" He beamed proudly. "You want a bump?"

"A who?" She asked getting turned on by both him and the mysterious substance.

"A bump, a line, come on," He invited seeing she still didn't get it.

"I'm warning you now, if I hit this it's gonna take me forever to cum." He advised as he made lines out of the shake.

"Take two then!" She blurted thinking about her quick draw husband and his quickest nut in the South.

"Yo ass finna be in trouble!" He warned and bent down to inhale a line into each nostril. "Here!" Teresa quickly accepted the rolled bill he used as a quill and snorted two lines before reason or good judgment could talk her out of it. As soon as the lines of pure cocaine disappeared up her nose she could have sworn she felt the earth move. She stopped just short of asking M.J. if he 'felt that'.

"Why are you here?" M.J. asked her peering into her soul. "Why did you come?"

"Because I want to have sex with you. I want you to fuck me," She admitted.

"That's what's up!" He nodded and lifted his shirt over his head. Before she could count his six pack he dropped his shorts. He wasn't hard yet but she was pleased with the large lump in his drawers.

Next it was his turn to be shocked as she lifted her dress over her head and was completely naked. He's dick instantly filled with blood giving him a stiff erection. M.J. proved true to his word that the coke kept him hard. It was over an hour and several positions later when he finally did cum.

The score on the orgasm card was her five to his one. He fucked her every which a way but loose. It wasn't until he placed her flat on her belly with her beautiful ass on display that he finally came. He pushed deep inside of her and skeeted on her cervix.

"Mmm that was good!" Teresa moaned, satisfied for the first time in years.

"Sho-nuff?" M.J. asked eagerly. He was hell on girls his age but this was a grown woman.

"Best I ever had." She blurted before she could catch herself. "I mean, it was okay."

"Uh huh too late!" M.J. laughed rolling off of her. "Say shawty, why you so tight? AnnaMaria's pussy way bigger than that!"

"Don't you mean Anna-Costa-Maria?" Teresa laughed. "You don't know your baby mama's name?"

"I never could say that shit!" M.J. confessed and chuckled. "Hell I can't even pronounce our sons name. It's Domirondo or Domodio or something like that. I just call that lil nigga 'D'."

"So what now?" Teresa sighed, seeking guidance. She needed to be told what to do. Her wimpy husbands yielding and submitting was a turn off.

"Shit next weekend!" He commanded. "And take some of that with you."

Teresa eagerly obeyed and put one of the bags containing 3.5 grams of cocaine into her purse. Once she made it home she put the cocaine with the blunt he had given her in the back of her panty drawer. A place Darrin would never look.

She would occasionally pull them out just to look at them. Just to savor the memory of how they made her feel, then put them back. Until one day she didn't.

Chapter 12

"Baby, please! Please don't leave me like this," Teresa begged as her husband headed to the shower. He had just broken her off with two minutes of loving and jumped up.

"Stop being so dramatic!" I'll only be gone for a week." He sighed. "This convention is too big for us to miss!"

"It's not your leaving or how long you'll be gone," she pleaded crawling to the edge of the bed as she spoke. "Don't leave me frustrated like this! Please baby make love to me right for once! Fuck me DAMMIT!"

"Why is that so important to you?" He spat with a look of pure disgust pasted on his face. "This is probably how you ended up in that 'situation' with Edwin!"

"Situation? You mean rape! Your precious friend RAPED ME!" She shot back incredulously.

She knew he and his long-time friend had been exchanging letters and her husband was sending him money. But this was the first indication of his doubting her story.

"Whatever it was, keep on this path you're gonna end up just like your mother!" He said shaking his head before closing the bathroom door behind him.

"My mother?" She repeated dangerously. "Did he just say my mother? I know this nigga did not just say my mother!"

The last time she heard from the woman who had birthed her was shortly after her wedding. Teresa couldn't even finish reading the excuse riddled letter. Nothing could excuse her running out on her family. Her daughter.

The first thing she wrote was; "It ain't easy being a preacher's wife." She crumpled it without going any further. Still, it was enough. It ain't easy being a preacher's wife.

Word around her daddy's church was that she and Michael were both on drugs living in a rundown motel.

"Look, I'm sorry," Darrin offered contritely once he showered. "It's just..."

"No, I'm fine. Enjoy your trip," She said so calmly. He should have known something was amiss. How men miss that tone is a mystery. Dude, if she was just 38 hot a second ago and she's calm and 'fine', she's about to fuck.

Darrin was so far out of tune with his wife he could not understand her needs. He couldn't know that her desperation stemmed in part from withdrawal from thorough fucking she received from her student. Guilt forced her to totally ignore M.J. The only time she said his name was roll call. Other than that she refused even eye contact.

Darrin shrugged his shoulders helplessly and finished packing. He blew his wife a half-hearted kiss from the door and left just like that, leaving her frustrated. She needed something, anything to get her through.

No it wasn't easy being a preacher's wife. Reverend Sanders hadn't even pulled all the way out of the driveway before she fished out the blunt from her panty drawer. By the time he left the sub-division she was exhaling the strong weed from her lungs.

"Mmm" Teresa moaned with pleasure from the soothing effects of the weed. It urged her to retrieve the baggie of cocaine as well. She stared at it for several minutes until it convinced her to use it. Twisted her arm and put a gun to her head screaming 'snort me!'

'Ok, just a little" she told it as she dumped more than 'just a little' onto a mirror. Teresa mimicked what M.J. did, crushing the little lumps into a powder and forming sortable lines.

'Just a little' she kept reminding herself as she snorted line after line. Just a little at a time until the supply was depleted. Teresa looked curiously at the empty baggie wondering where it all went.

The combination of weed and coke had her soaring! She felt fantastic, super, happy, and horny.

"I will do no such thing," she scolded herself out loud at the thought of masturbating to relieve her desires. Instead she picked up the phone.

"Oh, you 'member me now huh?" M.J. quipped actually feeling a little salty at being snubbed since their mid-day encounter.

"Listen are you coming to fuck me or not!" She demanded. "I have neither the time nor patience for the drama."

"How I get there?" he shot back. Since he didn't know how to operate the GPS in his vehicle, Teresa gave him old fashion directions. One of the directions was to bring more weed and coke.

"I got some weed but coke cost too much..." He began.

"Well bring it. I have money. Bring two hundred dollars-worth," she said spending what cash she knew to be on hand.

Teresa soaked in the tub as she awaited M.J.'s visit. An hour later he pulled up ghetto fabulously blasting music from his truck.

"Turn that off!" she demanded rushing out to the drive way. She now questioned the logic of inviting the thug to her home, as blinds along her otherwise quiet street open to investigate. Teresa whisked him inside in front of several sets of prying eyes.

"Did you bring it? The blow!" She asked eagerly. She instantly wished she could have retracted the statement after hearing the desperation in her tone.

M.J. heard it too. Accordingly he mentally reduced the quarter ounce he planned on selling for two hundred by half. That was still a discount because the customers he had in this part of town were still paying a hundred bucks a gram.

"Right here" M.J. smiled as he produced the package. "I doubled it up for you since Ima take a bump or two with you."

Once the coke was chopped and lined Teresa dove in face first. As she bent over to snort a line her ass peeked out of the small robe she wore.

"Damn shawty!" He exclaimed at the sight. He reached down and fondled her ass before sliding a finger into her wet vagina.

"Here! You do some too so you won't cum quickly!" She demanded fearful that he too might let her down.

"You ain't gotta worry about that! I sling this dick!" He bragged before complying. He passed her a rolled blunt and inhaled a few lines.

"Check this out." M.J. said pulling out his phone. He touched, tapped, and swiped until he found what he was looking for. Teresa looked at the screen and furrowed her brow as Annacostamaria expertly sucked his dick. He had advanced the video to ensure she saw him explode in her pretty face.

"And why pray-tell would you show me that?"

"So you can see how I like it." He shot back.

"I will not be performing oral sex on you!" She said indignantly.

"I feel you, so what's up? You want me to tighten you up before I push?" He asked indifferently.

"That's totally up to you" Teresa said using to her feet. Without another word she walked up to the steps and into the guest room with M.J. in tow.

Teresa climbed on the bed and removed what little she had on as M.J. stripped. He dropped his ghetto attire into a crumble heap on the floor before joining her on the bed. Four orgasms later, and Teresa's legs were jelly. M.J. literally 'beat it up' for her. Which is just what she expected.

Time for a little bump." She smiled inwardly. "Any more of the coke?" She inquired pleasantly.

"Naw, that's it" he lied smiling internally as well. He planned to milk more money out of her by selling her the other half of what she already paid for.

"Only got an eight-ball left but that's for a customer."

"Well you'll just have to sell it to me then," She insisted. "I'll write you a check."

"A check? Fuck I'm posed to do with a check? Dis a cash bizness!" M.J. frowned.

"Fine, just come through tomorrow and I'll pay you then." She instructed.

"No can do. I need the money tonight. I got things I need to do."

"Favor for a favor then" she smiled wickedly and cozied back up to him. It would be win/win if she could trick him out of another orgasm and the drugs.

"What you had in mind?" He asked beginning to stiffen at the prospect of fucking the gorgeous woman again.

"How bout I ride this monster?" She asked stroking him with her hand.

"Naw, I'm cool. I gotta see baby mama tonight," He replied. He knew full well that the mention of Annacostamaria would remind her of the blow job video. He was right and his teacher bent down to his crotch.

"How...about...I take...care of...this?" She asked between kisses and licks of his now rock hard dick.

"Mmm, I like that, do it like this," He said cueing baby mama back up. Teresa emulated what the young girl was doing until she found a rhythm of her own. Women automatically knew how to give head. It's in their DNA. Yeah I said it. So it wasn't hard to figure out.

M.J. hit the record button and began to film his teacher blowing him. Dealing with her quick drawn husband Teresa became an expert on gauging when a man was about to cum. She felt a surge and pulled him free from her mouth a millisecond before he exploded sending semen skyward.

"Mmm, you shoulda ate dat!" M.J. moaned.

Teresa just ignored him. She let him out after collecting her pay. As she snorted the blow she had mixed emotions about it. On one hand she just sucked a man's dick for drugs! On another hand it was fun.

Then on another hand the coke made it worth it. Good thing she had three hands.

The large amount of dick and dope quelled her thirst and desires for a while. Only for a while.

Chapter 13

Teresa could not be happier when summer finally arrived. She loved teaching but those inner-city kids were too much. The cursing, the yelling and fighting, the disrespect.

Yes summer was a welcome reprieve. Not to mention M.J's fine ass winking and blowing kisses every day. After their second episode she swore off both drugs and adultery. She had fun and got away with it but that wasn't her life. She was a preacher's wife.

The sex had improved at home, somewhat. Darrin still wouldn't or couldn't fuck for more than a few minutes at a time but she finally picked up that vibrator to handle the slack. All that was left was her addictive personality that could not be ignored, it had to be fed.

Most addicts are addicted more to the addiction than to any drug or activity. You have sex addicts, adrenaline junkies, drug, alcohol, you name it. Teresa turned to shopping. While her husband was out 'Reverending' she was burning down the malls and boutiques. It started off light as she initially only re-kindled her affair with shoes and purses. After spending all of her money she began dipping into the household funds. That went well for a while until the lights got cut off. Teresa had to scramble to get them turned back on before her husband came home.

A trip to daddy on the west side took care of that plus a few extra bucks that got spent before she made it home. Tired of robbing Peter to pay Paul, Teresa took out a small loan with her stellar credit. That lasted a couple of weeks before it was gone. When she ran out of room in the closets, for all of the clothes, she began stashing her purchases in the garage. A new credit card came in the mail every week and was maxed out shortly after. Something had to give. Something did.

"Teresa!" Darrin boomed from the garage. The sheer horror in his voice indicated the gig was up. "Get out here this instant!"

"Oh shit!" She sighed knowing the shit had just hit the floor. "Here we go."

She was still thinking of excuses when she reached the garage. Darrin had a look of bewilderment pasted on his face as he stacked shoes and purses into a pile.

"Oh my God!" He moaned when he discovered the bins filled with clothes and trinkets, most still with the tags attached.

"Baby, I can explain!" She said as a lie about a charity formed in her mind.

'Maybe not' Teresa thought when Darrin opened the freezer and an avalanche of shoes tumbled towards him.

The grand total was just north of one hundred thousand dollars. That was only the merchandise that he found. They were able to return half of the items but were stuck with the rest. That's when Darrin found out that their entire savings was gone and that the new and existing credit cards were maxed out and overdue.

"I'll have to get it from the church." Darrin sighed. "I can borrow it from one of the petty cash accounts."

"The church has that much in petty cash?" She exclaimed. She knew the congregation was affluent and broke bread but fifty grand was far from petty.

What she didn't know yet was that they had hit the big league. Plans for mega church complex complete with a dome, school, gym, etc. were in the works. The petty cash account was petty even though it held three times that amount.

"I'll take care of this but two things must happen!" Darrin began in a tone she had never heard from her husband. "One, you will pay the money back. Every cent! And two this can never ever happen again!"

"Ok baby, I'm sorry," Teresa offered contritely. "I'll pay it all back and I'll make it up to you."

"How can you possibly make it up to me?" He demanded. "What can you do to fix this mess?"

For response Teresa walked over and knelt in front of her husband. Darrin watched with a curious frown as she unzipped his pants and pulled out his penis. He damn near went into shock when she put it into her mouth. He was so outraged he reeled back and slapped her away.

"What has gotten into you!" He screamed.

"Did you just hit me?" Teresa asked confused by the stinging of her cheek. "You slapped me?"

"Yes I did!" I did not marry a Jezebel! A harlot, did I? Repent! Repent!" He repeated as he retreated.

It was days later before they spoke again. Darrin did apologize and Teresa claimed to accept it but the relationship would never be the same again. She no longer loved her husband but she would not follow in her mother's footsteps and leave her home. The couple drifted apart by the day only going through the motions.

She cooked and cleaned, and he occasionally spent a few minutes inside of her. The mood was so subdued. The marriage so strained Teresa was livid to find out she was pregnant.

****

"This cannot be!" Teresa whined at the pink plus sign she just peed on. "That man won't fuck me for but a few seconds at a time and I'm pregnant!"

If she hadn't been careless she would have gotten an abortion. And Darrin would have never known. Instead she left the positive test strip in the trash can where he found it. He was oddly ecstatic.

"We're having a baby?" He screamed holding the test stick like the Olympic torch. He picked his wife up and twirled her around in joy. There went her appointment for an abortion she had planned to sneak and do without his knowledge. His visits to her vagina were so infrequent, he would have never known.

"I'm praying for a boy!" He yelled before dropping down and doing just that. At the same time she prayed to miscarry.

Teresa tried to accept the fact that she was just another sexually frustrated wife. A large number of women are married to men who simply can't satisfy them. Sure they are good providers, great dads, etc. but the dick game was zero. It is what it is.

******

Teresa began the next semester teaching in the high school in the same affluent county she lived in. The ghetto kids were bad, horrible in fact, but these spoiled rich kids were worse. The brats dabbled in more debauchery than their counterparts in the inner-city.

All day she heard conversations about blow jobs or who was screwing who. To make matters worse no one was screwing her. Not being able to sneak some weed or pop a pill due to her pregnancy only made matters worse. That meant she had to deal with her problems head on, sober. And being the selfish, spoiled Prima Donna that she was, it was killing her.

Teresa threw herself at her husband night after night, and night after night he rejected her. Although she was only a couple of months and not even showing yet, Darrin was convinced sex would harm the baby.

"Baby you won't be inside me long enough to harm anything" she spat in frustration.

"Sex, sex, sex, sex! That's all I hear out of you!" Darrin spat back. "I swear I feel like I married a whore at times."

"A what?" Teresa demanded, leaping from the bed. "Did you just call me a whore!"

"You need to calm down! Why don't you take a cold shower or go for a walk or drive." He said dismissively.

"You know what? You right!" Teresa nodded. She pulled on a pair of sweats over the sexy lingerie set that, failed to entice her husband, "I do need some air."

"Have fun!" Darrin shouted at her back as she left the room, then house. Teresa hit the highway like a woman on a mission. In fact she was. Teresa cursed her decision to delete the number as she sped across town in hopes he would be in the same place. Luckily for her M.J. really was dumb enough to still use the same hotel as his headquarters.

"Yessssss!!!" Teresa exclaimed pumping her delicate fist at the sight of M.J.'s truck in the lot.

"Our boy has it going on tonight," Detective Walker said watching yet another pretty woman rush to the room. "That's the second one."

"One for each of us," His partner in crime, Detective Pittman agreed.

"Mrs. Sanders?" M.J. asked at the sight of his teacher at the door.

"Surprise! You know I had to come back for some of that good .... Oh hey Annacostamaria!" Teresa exclaimed, switching gears upon seeing baby mama sprawled across the bed.

"Hey ma'am" she replied cheerfully.

"Some good what?" M.J. smiled rubbing his hand up and down his shirtless torso.

Needlessly embarrassed at the presence of the mother of his child, Teresa pointed to the cocaine on the table. In an instant her focus had switched. She now had to have some of the drug. Both would be nice but if forced to choose....

Teresa's mind flashed to her unborn and unformed child as she inhaled her first line of coke. By the time she hit the next it was the furthest thing from her mind.

"You must be shopping?" M.J. asked eagerly.

"Well actually I hadn't planned on it and neglected to bring any money," She admitted sheepishly. M.J. spoke that and heard what she didn't say.

"Say umm.... Anna-Ria, let's have us a threesome," he announced pushing a little more coke in front of the teacher.

"Okaaaaay" Annacostamaria sang joyfully. The eager young girl would have had the same reply no matter what was asked of her.

"Wanna rob a bank?" "Okaaaaay",

"Fly to the moon?" "Okaaaaaay",

"Have sex with our teacher?" "Okaaaay"

The girl was as close to brain dead as one could be and still have a pulse. Buzzing from the strong coke, and sex starved, Teresa joined her on the bed. She quickly peeled off the sweats to the delights of her host.

"Shit!" M.J. exclaimed at the revealing bra and thong.

"That's nice" Annacostamaria sang as she pulled the wife beater over her head. As soon as Teresa removed her wet thong the girl took its place.

"Oh my!" Teresa jumped when her tongue found its destination. She came in seconds.

"My turn!" Annacostamaria giggled and lay back granting her teacher access. Teresa didn't even hesitate in returning the favor. She had never done it before but the young girl's moans directed her which way to go.

M.J. scrambled to record the episode on his phone. Once his girl-friend thrashed around from her own orgasm he couldn't take any more. He quickly dropped his shorts and rammed himself into the preacher's wife. A few seconds later he pounded them both to an or-gasm. A few seconds after that the motel door swung open.

"What do we have here?" Walker asked despite the obvious.

"Looks like one of them umm Nikki Minaj things," Pittman croaked.

"Whoa!" Walker warned whipping out his pistol in response to M.J.'s sudden move.

"Easy officer, just getting my shawts," he said stopping and raising his hands.

Pittman checked the pockets and removed a wad of cash before handing them over.

"You holding out on us Michael," Walker chided. "My car note is overdue thanks to you."

"Shit been slow shawty, that's five stacks right there," M.J. replied sounded wounded.

"That's a start," Pittman said verifying then splitting the money.

"I'll take a little of that dome," he said looking at Teresa who was attempting to cover herself with a pillow.

"Yeah I'll have some myself," Walker added.

"Chill she ain't 'bout that life, my girl will hook y'all up," M.J. pleaded.

"Let me see some ID," Pittman demanded as Annacostamaria began blowing his partner. He copied all the information from her driver's license to his pad. Once the first cop grunted filling her mouth with cum the second one took his place and did the same.

"Get the rest of that money to us like yesterday," Walker demanded as they prepared to leave.

"See ya later umm miss .... no Mrs. Sanders," Pittman said with a wink.

"I'm sorry about that Mrs. Sanders," M.J. said sincerely. To prove it he handed her a bag of cocaine. Teresa was livid beyond words as she struggled to comprehend what just happened. An hour ago she was safe and sound in her home, with her husband, now she just witnessed a shakedown, gun drawn, and blow job bribe.

"I, I, I have to go," she stammered as she rushed back into her clothes. She absent mindedly clutched to coke as she drove away.

"No more! No more sex! No more drugs!" She ordered her reflection in the rear view. She raced home to rejoin her life.

Chapter 14

After the close call in the hotel room, Teresa was too done with the streets. She put M.J. and his good loving to the back of her mind and left him there. The only problem now was that damn blow.

Teresa had no idea why she even took it, let alone brought it home. She tucked it away in her secure panty drawer but it was running her crazy. It literally demanded her attention but the fetus inside her deterred her from using. Instead she would pull it out and toy with it. She would dump a little out onto a mirror and make perfect lines but wouldn't snort them. She romanced the glistening powder until it finally won.

"I am in my third trimester," she agreed before bending over to snort a line. Then another. The long awaited high was like blast off! Like the Apollo, Atlantis and America all taking off at once.

Before she knew it the mirror was empty. Her body was on auto-pilot as if controlled by something else, as she dumped more coke out of the bag. The drug stirred her other desires causing her to take a break to masturbate. The dildo did what Darrin would not and honestly could not. Since she could literally fuck herself she said fuck him. Pride prevented her from begging for the sexual scraps he could spare her. She let him have her when he wanted but that wasn't very often.

Teresa had mixed emotions once the cocaine was depleted. On one hand it could harm her baby. On the other, it was risky, get caught sneaking hits while her husband slept beside her.

'Look at this sorry ass nigga' she fumed looking down at her snoring, slobbering husband.

Regular life was so mundane. Up at six, cook breakfast, eat, shower, dress, work, home, cook, eat, listen to 'Reverend can't fuck' practice a sermon, tv, sleep, repeat. It was killing her. Then, Teresa gave birth.

When she first gazed into her daughter's eyes the name Hazel popped into her head and then found its way onto the birth certificate.

Darrin of course insisted on a more biblical name. Like Praise, or Glory to go along with his own mother's name. But Teresa said fuck him, no way was she calling her child Glory-Earline.

Having a child consumed all her time and energy. It chases the demon of drug addiction into far recesses of her busy mind. Teresa decided to be a stay at home mom to spend every second with her baby.

Seconds turned to days, months, and years. The next time Teresa looked up Hazel was ready for school. Watching your first child board that bus, on the first day of school, gives a sense of melancholy like nothing else. An anxious mix of fear and elation.

The fear wasn't for her child because she knew the fussy, demanding little Prima-Donna could hold her own. Teresa was afraid for herself; of herself what would she do now with all that time on her hands. The demons began stirring the second the school bus left her sight. Of course they had a plan for her free time. The last five years were spent catering to Princess Hazels every whim. She doted on her child so much so, that even at five Teresa still referred to her as the 'baby'.

Restlessness drove Teresa out into the world in search of distractions. She wandered around town, burning huge amounts of gas in her new SUV when she ended up on Atlanta's West Side. She decided to pop in and see Sister Clarice.

Clarice and her dad married ages years back when the murmurs of Pastor's live-in girlfriend grew audible. Like they forgot that Pastors got needs.

"Oh, hey chile!" Clarice exclaimed so happily it gave Teresa pause. She quickly un-furrowed her brow and smiled back.

"Hey Sister Clarice," she said exchanging a warm hug. That's when she smelled the vodka. The two women made congenial small talk as Teresa secretly pined for a sip of her own. When none was offered she finally asked.

"Is that alcohol Sister Clarice?!" She asked feigning surprise.

"Chile, it ain't easy being a preacher's wife," she sighed. Ole Rev had starting spreading a little dick with the Gospel again.

"I'm a preachers wife too you know," came the reply.

"Grab you a glass out of the cupboard," Clarice laughed producing a pint bottle from the sofa cushion. Teresa had a nice buzz when she pulled away from her childhood home. Nothing serious, just a warm glow that made her smile. She was happy again. On a whim she drove up the long way on Cascade, or as her mother use to call it the wrong way.

Old memories filled her mind as the landscape turned from manicured to ghetto. Curiosity turned the truck onto Leticia and Dante's street. The plan was to drive by slowly and inhale some memories, but.

"That cannot be!" Teresa marveled at the sight of her old friend sitting on the porch. She pulled into the driveway and rushed to greet her old friend. It reminded her of the fact that she had no new friends.

"Gurl is dat you!" Leticia slurred ghetto as ever.

'Girl is that you!' Teresa thought upon closer inspection of her long lost friend. She still wore the same 'hoochie mama' clothes complete with 'booty shorts' and cheap sandals. Her hair was braided up ghetto fabulously.

"Hey girl" Teresa sang as they embraced. It was at that moment she realized just how lonely she really was.

"Chile I ain't seent you in a thousand days! Let me see you!" Leticia announced breaking the hug. "Gurl you look good!"

"Chile you too!" Teresa lied. "And you killing them shorts."

"Thank ya!" Leticia said doing a spin so her friend could see her. All Teresa saw were the five boys running in and out of the house. The first thought was that perhaps her friend ran a daycare from the house. That notion was dispelled when they all called her 'mama'.

"Dese my boys" Leticia said proudly. Attempting to coral the rambunctious boys for introduction, when that failed she pointed at them and relayed their colorful names.

"Dis MarkTavious, dat dere is Dontavious, that one is Saga...Shaqu... wait ... Shaquilliam", she said as a snotty nosed, hyper-active child sped past.

"I never could say dat shit! Oh and der go my twins cash and money," Leticia beamed as the little boy sped past on all fours and scrambled up a tree like a set of spider monkeys. "My daughter Shanadoa wit hur daddy."

"Wow!" Teresa exclaimed at the amount of kids she had as well as the shock of her friend's appearance. She was even more ghetto than she recalled.

"MarkTavious! Brang mama a beer! Two!" Leticia ordered her oldest son/bartender.

The little boy knew how to fix a few drinks already and could roll a blunt like nobody's business.

"You want a beer?"

"Um, sure." Teresa agreed as Leticia produced a blunt from her cheap purse.

She indulged in both and the demons were happy. Content, for now.

'*Mmm I feel sooooo good*' Teresa smiled internally. The weed and alcohol had her feeling mellow. All that was missing was some good dick.

"Let's see if I can trick ole Rev out of some wood," Teresa laughed and pressed down on the gas pedal. Hazel frowned at the shortened bedtime story but that was all she had coming. Mama was on a mission. She showered, lotioned, and dressed in a yellow pair of boy shorts and matching bra. Darrin was already in bed studying for his next sermon as his wife slinked in. The effects of the alcohol and weed had waned, now pure lust propelled her. She was in heat.

"Eh... Excuse me Darrin, but does this color look good on me?" She asked sweetly.

Teresa turned sideways to give a good view of her plump ass cheeks hanging out of the bottom of the boy shorts. Darrin was initially perturbed at the interruption until he looked up and ass filled his vision.

"Yes Lawd!" He murmured sitting his books down. "Let me see that." Teresa came close and let him marvel at her backside as if just discovering it. Like he just realized his wife had ass. Darrin reached out tentatively and touched softly.

She slowly peeled it off enjoying the look of awe on his face. And the feel of his touch. It had been months since he last rolled over on top of her in the middle of the night. She always felt a mix of emotions when he sexed her like that. On one hand she knew it was only because he wanted and needed release. On the other hand she was grateful for any contact with her husband. Tonight would be different she thought. Tonight Darrin would make slow, passionate, lengthy love to her. She stripped completely as he removed his pajama pants.

"Mmm, Teresa moaned taking his rock hard dick into her hand. She massaged her clit with the head before guiding him inside. The couple traded friendly kisses as he slowly eased inside.

Darrin pushed deep inside of her until he reached the bottom. Then, his whole body went rigid as he came inside of her with a grunt. He didn't last one stroke!

"No you didn't! You selfish son of a bitch!" Teresa growled.

"Girl your mouth!" Darrin exclaimed looking down at her.

"My mouth? Your damn dick nigga! Get the fuck off of me!" She yelled pushing him out and off of her.

"I don't understand? We just had sex." He complained confused by the outburst.

"Want something done you gotta do it your damn self." Teresa mumbled as she rummaged in her nightstand.

"What the Sam Hill is that?" Reverend asked when the dildo came out. For a reply she turned the dial filling the room with a gentle hum. She worked her clit with the vibrator for a minute before inserting it.

"What the world!" Darrin exclaimed as his wife fucked herself.

"Fuck!" She screamed as an orgasm wracked her body.

Darrin alternated between asking silly questions and praying over her as she recovered from the strong sensation. She would have gone again if he would have shut the fuck up. Instead she ignored him and put the wet vibrator on the night stand.

She had made up her mind, no more hiding. If she wanted to get off, she would, right in front of him. He of course would be praying for her while she did. One night he got the gal to snatch it out of her and insert himself in its place. The show of force turned Teresa on but unfortunately he didn't last a full minute.

That was the proverbial straw that broke the camel's back. She needed some dick and decided to go out and get some.

Chapter 15

"You go girl!" Teresa told her reflection in the clubs glass window.

She still couldn't believe she was actually there but she was. Darrin prayed then berated her as she got dressed for her night out. He called her a 'loose woman' when she slipped into the tiny red dress.

It was just fuel to the fire. Teresa was far too spoiled to be denied what she wanted. She could not and would not take no for an answer.

"Hey pretty lady," A pretty man said flashing a brilliant smile.

Teresa nodded with approval as she inspected him up and down. He stood a solid six feet tall and had a head full of pretty, curly brown hair that matched his light eyes. She shot a glance down to his feet and smiled at their size.

"Hey yourself" she replied having made up her mind that he would do. She would fuck him. "I'm Teresa"

"Calvin. Care for a drink?" He asked politely.

"Actually I'm looking for dick. I need to be fucked," She blurted, surprising the man. "Let's cut to the chase, I want sex, not made love to, not a quickie, I need you to tear the walls down. Can you handle that?"

"Can I! Lady this is your lucky night!" He smiled.

"Well let's see what you're working with," Teresa said and grabbed his crotch. Calvin instantly stiffened in her hand, pleasing her immensely. This was the first time she had been eaten since Annacostamaria some years back, and she came instantly. Calvin was generous enough to lick and suck her to another orgasm before pushing inside of her.

Calvin gave her the business from different positions and angles for close to an hour. He had a rhythmic stroke as if music was playing in his head. After bringing her to multiple orgasms he final had one of his own. He pushed deep inside of her and filled her with semen.

"Thank you so much" Teresa said cordially as if he had just helped bring her groceries to her car. In a way, he did. She tapped his side gently, telling him to get up. Calvin pulled his deflating penis out of her and lay on his back.

"So write your number down. We can hook up again sometime," He offered casually.

"No, I don't think my husband would approve. In fact I'm sure he wouldn't. Being a preacher and all," She chuckled as she dressed.

"You're married!" Calvin exclaimed sitting up on his bed.

"Very," she said holding up her ring finger to show the dazzling display of ice Darrin gave her more for the benefit of him than her. He looked so dejected sitting there with his lip poked out, she almost felt sorry for him. Almost.

*****

Darrin didn't question his wife when she came home from her girls' night out however, he did check her panties when she went back into the shower. Good thing for both of them she changed from the cum filled pair in the garage, and left them in the truck. The effect of a good dicking down lasted a couple months. Rev filled in the blanks when he could but the couple grew distant.

They maintained separate lives in the same house. Teresa could only laugh when she realized she was pregnant. Realized wasn't the right word, accepted is more like it. She hadn't had a period since before her night out on the town. Ole Rev must have knocked her up during one of his late night drive-by fuckings.

"I'm pregnant," Teresa announced dryly when her husband joined her in bed.

"Excuse me!" Darrin exclaimed, pulling off his glasses as if that would make him hear better.

"You heard me," she said without hostility. She knew he heard her and didn't feel like repeating herself.

He jumped for joy and gave an un-reciprocated hug. Darrin had been hinting that he would love to have a son. An heir to carry the

Sanders' name on once he was gone. To his credit he did try. He made every effort to please his miserable wife. When that failed he set out to placate her but fell short there as well.

Teresa had a chip on her shoulder that she couldn't shake off. Deep down she knew what was eating her. She needed to get high. Nothing heavy, just little weed. Something to take the edge off. Once that was settled she jumped into her truck and headed over to the West Side. She smiled at the sight of her friend sitting on the front steps as she pulled up. Thought it luck or good timing but truth be told as a welfare queen that was her post. Weather permitting Leticia could be found there, on the job at least eight hours a day. Sitting there watching life unfold in front of her instead of taking an active role in it.

"Hey gurl!" Leticia called out warmly as Teresa dismounted the truck.

"Hey yourself" she replied as she plucked a smoldering blunt from her fingers. She took a huge drag that made Leticia want to snatch it back. The effects of the sweets buds were immediate. As the THC soaked into her brain. A smile spread across her face as the drug confirmed her suspicions. This is what was missing from her life.

They politely fought over the blunt pulling it out of each other's hand until it was gone. Teresa couldn't remember feeling this good in a while. A long while.

"Do you have any more of that? I would like some to take home," Teresa asked sweetly.

"Gurrrrl no! And it's dat fiyah! I ain't got no money until my check come and 'Danny Boy' don't take no credit. Won't even take no head," Leticia frowned.

"Well I have cash, call this... 'Danny-Boy' person and make a purchase," Teresa said very businesslike. "How much can this get us?"

"Plenty!" Leticia screamed at the sight of the hundred dollar bill. She whipped out her cell phone so quickly it was like a magic trick.

"Say shawty bring me a half and a fiddy," she said excitedly knowing her prissy friend didn't speak hood.

A couple of minutes filled with inane small talk later, a very handsome yet extremely ghetto young man pulled up in a decked out old Chevy. The bass from the car's system shook Teresa's digestive track with every kick of the drums. Even after coming to a complete stop. The huge rims just kept spinning.

"Sup shawty" Danny Boy smiled wider than necessary. But when you have that many gold teeth in your mouth you want everyone to see it. Isn't that the point? Or do people get gold teeth to chew better? To be able to bite harder?

"Come on in da house" Leticia said grabbing the money from Teresa. Once inside she purchased a half an ounce of Kush and a fifty of crack.

"You always tryna shawt a nigga," Danny Boy complained.

"Shit come by later and I'll give you some head," Leticia bartered as she took half of Teresa's weed from the bag.

"That's what up!" Danny Boy smiled before turning to leave. He was definitely coming back, definitely!

"Wow that's a lot" Teresa said ignorantly when she received the bag of fluffy weed.

"Yeah he be hooking me up," she replied. "Break me off a little." Teresa figured it out that she was requesting some of the weed and gave her half of what she had. She just paid one hundred bucks for an eighth of an ounce.

"I really shouldn't be doing this. I'm pregnant again," Teresa confided.

It was one of those times when you admit something to someone so they can talk you out of it.

"Whut! Girl me too!" Leticia yelled, lifting her shirt to show her slightly producing belly. "Chile I done smoked with all my kids and day fine!"

As soon as the words left her mouth the twins burst from the house. The shirtless boys hit a gorilla roll and scrambled up the tree.

"See!" Leticia said proudly.

That of course almost made her give her friend the rest of the weed. Instead she thought back to the coke binges she had while carrying Hazel. Her child was perfect in every regard.

"Girl I hope dis Marco baby," Leticia said wistfully. "The rest of dem niggas ain't shit."

Teresa could only shake her head. Imagine not knowing who the father of your child was.

Chapter 16

"It's a boy!" The doctor exclaimed as the eight pound infant was pulled free from her vagina.

"A boy! A boy!" Darrin cheered through his mask. "Thank you baby, thank you!"

"You're welcome dear," Teresa replied. She craned her neck to get a view of her son but he was being cleaned and checked.

"Calvin?" She gasped when the curly headed miniature version of her one night stand was placed on her chest.

"Calvin?" Hmm Calvin Sanders." Darrin nodded. "Nice ring to it, Calvin Sanders it is."

Of course that's not what she meant but there was no way of explaining. Teresa saw the look in her husband's eyes and knew she would never tell him his son wasn't his. This was one of those secrets you took to the grave with you.

No, it was not fair to the child to not let him know who his father was. Nor was it fair to Darrin to let him dote over a child who was not his. It probably wasn't fair to Calvin either to not inform him that he had a child. Only it wasn't about them, it was about her. It's not easy being a preacher's wife.

******

Over the next few years Reverend and Mrs. Sanders' income and prestige had grown tremendously along with the congregation. The mega church and compound was complete. Along with a mini-mansion for the pastor. And of course Pastor can't be seen pushing no bullshit, so he was gifted a top of the line Benz. He upgraded his wife's SUV as well.

The Sanders were now southern Baptist royalty. Teresa played her position by taking a position in the church, to take an active role in affairs of the church. Affairs of the church is right because everybody was fucking everybody!

Deacon Johnson fucked half the senior choir, while junior Pastor Smith fucked the other half. Sister Bethel was rumored to have the best head south in the Mason Dixie Line. Sister Melody had kids by nine members of the church. Teresa overlooked the shenanigans until it hit close to home. Until it came to the pastor's secretary.

Anita was fresh out of Reverend and Mrs. Own Alma Mata. She was twenty two, beautiful, well built, and in love with the preacher. Teresa had caught her flirting shamelessly with him on several occasions. Anita was bubbly and friendly with everybody but shut down as soon as she walked into the room.

Anita also dressed right on the verge of being inappropriate. Teresa could not care less if her husband had a girlfriend, fuck him. The woman in her however insisted she check the chick.

"Umm excuse me umm, Amanda?" Teresa began.

"Anita!" She checked hotly.

"Well yes, anyway. The pastor is married. To me. His wife," she laid out plainly thinking that should be enough.

"And? So!" Anita said curtly. "I know who you are!"

Teresa was taken aback by her tone. At first she didn't entertain the notion that her husband was seeing the woman. If he wouldn't fuck her he certainly wouldn't fuck his secretary. *So why be catty?*

"Well since you know who I am make sure, damn sure you stay out of his face! Unless you want me in yours!" Teresa said hotly.

"Whatever!" She sang with a juvenile wave of her hand and rolling of the neck and eyes.

"Whatever? Bit..."

"What's going out here?" Reverend Sanders asked coming out of the office just before Teresa got to complete the threat.

"Your wife!" Anita said as if the word had a foul taste to it. "Is trying to check me! Please talk to her Darrin."

"Darrin? Don't you mean Reverend Sanders?" Teresa spat to her husband.

Darrin looked back and forth between the two women as if he was unsure what to do.

"Anita, go into my office. Teresa we'll talk at home," He finally decided.

She was in shock. She just stood there with her mouth agape after her husband followed his secretary into the office.

She was on 85 south doing 85 miles per hour when she snapped back to reality. Her body was on auto-pilot as she switched lanes to the 75 South exit. Her destination was The Hood.

It had been years since she last ventured into Atlanta's notorious South West Side, but there she was. Every time she got stressed she felt the urge to get high. She always fought it. Until now.

It seemed as if things had stayed the same in the ghetto. As if time stopped in the hood. The same addicts were posted up in front of the same stores. The same skinny crack whores directions traffic.

When she pulled onto her friend's block there was Leticia on her post. Judging from the small army of children around, she had been fruitful and multiplied. Times two!

"Gurl, is dat you!" Leticia jumped up and slurred as Teresa stepped down from the truck.

"Tis I," Teresa replied playfully as she embraced her musty friend.

"Please tell me you have a blunt?" Teresa pleaded.

"I got half a one, but it's dirty," She replied.

"Dirty, clean it doesn't matter," She urged having no idea what she was agreeing to. She was about to find out real quick.

When Leticia lit the blunt it sizzled loudly under the flame causing Teresa to take notice. She marveled at the way her friend's eyes grew wide as she inhaled deeply. A look of euphoria spread across her face, similar to the satisfied look of an orgasm.

Teresa was almost afraid as she took the cigar from Leticia's trembling hand. She took a long, slow, tentative pull and felt the effects immediately. The crack cocaine smoke raced through every cell in her body, implanting its presence in her being, forever.

It was pissing on trees, marking its turf. It had staked its claim and now owned a piece of her. If she never hit it ever again in life she would always remember the first hit. But hit it again she did. Hit it so hard Leticia became envious.

"Take it easy shawty!" Leticia complained. "That's my last!" Teresa passed the dwindling blunt back and held the smoke as long as she possibly could. Held it for dear life before responding.

"Call your person. I would like to make a purchase," She ordered as if short on office supplies.

Leticia made the call and a few minutes later a young dealer pulled up and delivered the weed and cocaine. She stared curiously at the little blue bags that contained her future along with the small rocks inside. It was at that moment the magnitude of what she was about to embark on became evident. This was crack!

National News had been running reports of an Atlanta man named Willie Champion who was recently found dead. He had been one of the most promising athletes in the history of the city until becoming strung out on drugs. His heart breaking life story was now being called "CHRONICLES OF A JUNKY".

He was destroyed by the same substance she now held precariously in her palm. Her hundred dollar bill purchased ten of the small bags, which judging by Leticia's elation was a big deal. When Teresa handed her five of the bags she passed wind loudly from excitement.

"Thank you, thank you so much!" She exclaimed on the verge of tears as she embraced her. "I love you gurl!"

"Well your quite welcome," Teresa chuckled, "Can you fix us another one please?"

"Sho nuff! Give me one of your sacks," Leticia said intending on saving hers.

Teresa took mental notes as she crushed the crack, crumbled the weed and emptied a cigar. She then deftly reassembled all the ingredients into the cigar and sealed it with saliva.

"Shaquilliam! Brang mama a beer! And don't you drank nare sip!" Leticia called out.

Teresa felt an uneasy yearning waiting for her friend to light the blunt.

"I'll do the honors!" Teresa said snatching the blunt away and lighting it. She took a few healthy pulls before grudgingly passing it to her friend in exchange for a swig of cold malt liquor. The women alternated sips for pulls until both sources of stimuli were gone.

"Gimme another bag I'll roll us one mo!" Leticia demanded with an outstretched palm.

"I must be getting home now," Teresa replied. She had enough of sharing. She wanted to smoke alone in the privacy of her own home. It was all she could do to obey the speed limit hoping to beat the school bus home.

Chapter 17

"I'll hook you up but you gotta give me two hundred dollars!" Leticia huffed. She had been hitting her up for half of whatever she bought but seeing the desperation she decided to straight up extort her.

"To call your friend! Are you serious?" Teresa exclaimed.

"Mm hmm cuz lil Boobie got some bullshit and M.J. don't sell anything under a quarter." Leticia said moving her head from side to side. The ball was in her court and she knew it.

"Did you say M.J.?" Teresa asked, as memories of his dick flashed into her mind.

"Mm hmm and he got dat fiyah!"

"Call him!" Teresa yelled.

She felt moisture seep into her frilly panties when the M.J. she knew pulled up in the same custom truck he had for years. Of course it was in stellar condition and tricked out with all the latest etceteras.

"Is that you?" M.J. shouted at the sight of his former teacher.

"It is!" She smiled at the sight of her former lover. It had been nine years since their last episode. She stopped dealing with him after the incident in the hotel.

"This is for you?" He asked ready to make the sale.

"Friend of mine actually, I ..."

"Uh huh! It's hurs!" Leticia chimed I'm attempting to cock block. "M.J. don't mess with no smokers!"

"Here go my number," M.J. offered ignoring the hater. He jotted down his digits on the back of a receipt and handed it to Teresa.

Afterwards he sold her a quarter ounce each of crack and weed. A smile and a wink served as good-bye and he was gone.

"Oooh gurl, he like you," Leticia said switching back to friend mode. Her black mail plan was short lived and she knew it.

"Good bye," Teresa smirked and turned to leave.

Desperately Leticia moved aggressively towards Teresa to retrieve some drugs.

"I don't think so," she replied and prepared for battle. Teresa tensed for the first fight of her life.

"So, let's smoke one den," Leticia smiled, backing down. "I'll grab us a beer."

By the time she returned with the beer Teresa was halfway up the street. Leticia wanted to give chase but didn't. It would be years next time they saw each other. By then both of their lives would be drastically different.

Teresa raced to her father's house to claim her children so she could get home and get high. Of course they didn't want to leave, and then her dad came in and wanted to talk about everything! It was hours before she finally made it home. And wouldn't you know it before she could get up to her sanctuary, little Calvin wanted a juice box. Her addictive personality had passed along to her son. Dude was a juice box junky.

"Speaking of juice boxes," Teresa said she finally exhaled her first hit.

She dialed M.J.'s number and slipped her free hand into her panties. She played in her own juice box as it rang.

"Who dis?" M.J. barked loud enough to be heard over the thunderous D-Lite bouncing around in his truck.

"The correct phrase is, who, is this. I'll give you one guess."

"Hmp, teacher lady!" He smiled reducing the volume. "You calling for some hard or you want some hard?"

"Both! Talk nasty to me," she whined.

"Like what? Like how you wanna ride the big dick?" He asked wickedly as an erection rose in his pants.

"Mmm yeah I wanna ride that ...."

"Mother!" Hazel called out while simultaneously knocking on the door, "Amber is here, can I go to the mall with her?"

"Ain't this some shit!" She fumed inwardly while removing her wet fingers from herself. "Go on! I'm coming to see you!" She whispered.

"Business or pleasure?" M.J. asked, eager for both.

"Both!"

*****

It took a week before Teresa actually was able to create a window to link up with M.J. It happened to coincide with the depletion of her drugs. She figured she would fill both needs as once.

It took some fussing and demanding to get her husband to spend time with his own children. She took a lot of shit in her life with the kids, the congregation, and loveless marriage. She will be damned if she couldn't get her some 'me time'.

As usual she met M.J. at a nondescript motel. And as usual the sex was outrageous. It had been close to a year since her husband last graced her vagina with his presence. M.J. felt the benefits of that absence.

"Damn shawty you tight!" he grunted after climaxing in a few strokes. "You turned back into a virgin."

Before Teresa had a chance to complain, he flipped her over and fucked the day-lights out of her. She lost count after her fourth orgasm and took what he had to offer. Since she was a far cry from the ghetto hood rats and occasional crack whores he fucked, he was having as much fun as she was.

"Mmm that should get me a discount," Teresa laughed as M.J. collapse on her back out of breath.

"That's what's up," he managed to say as he caught his breath. "Wait, you smoking now?"

"Yes!" She exclaimed shamelessly. Her world was so far removed from the hood she didn't see the devastating effects of crack.

In fact hers was one of the few black families in America that had not been touched by addiction. Until now that is.

"I just love the feeling! It makes me soar!" She sang as she slipped back into her panties and bra.

She stopped short of getting fully dressed so she could get one for the road. M.J. just shook his head.

'What a waste' he thought to himself. Here was this beautiful, intelligent, professional black woman smoking yams. She could not last. No one does.

'May as well eat off this bitch' he shrugged. Since she was playing around with dirty blunts he decided to promote her so she would spend more money, more often.

"Here, try this!" M.J. offered politely.

"What is it?" Teresa asked staring curiously at the glass tube before reaching for it.

She examined the burnt end and scratched at the Brillo stuffed in the end.

"It's a shooter. You wasting your time with them blunts." He explained.

As he spoke he fixed her a nice solid hit. Not enough to stop her heart but enough to ensure she was hooked. Love at first blast.

Teresa inhaled as directed, slowly and deeply as the powerful drug sped from the tip of the pipe straight into her soul. The evil smoke filled her lungs and seeped into her subconscious. When she blew out that first hit, along with it went all that wouldn't do.

M.J. stalled for a while before fixing her another. He needed her to feel the up and down of the drug she knew up was better. After sexing her once more he graciously allowed her to keep the shooter. That along with an ounce of hard that he graciously over-charged her for.

He knew she would be back. It was now official, Teresa was a junky.

Chapter 18

"Can't be right?" Teresa frowned at the ATM error message. It was only the second week of the month; no way was the monthly household account dry. No way has she spent $4,000 dollars that fast. While a good portion actually did go to the family's lavish upkeep, M.J. got the rest.

He both shorted and overcharged her at the same time. Her 'ounces' cost a thousand dollars and only weighed scant fifteen grams. To top it off M.J. sexually taxed her on every visit. Teresa didn't mind because Darrin didn't touch her at all now. He even stopped rolling over into her in the middle of the night. For her it was a win/win, get high and fucked.

With her own money gone Teresa had no choice but to hit one of the church accounts. Since she personally handled several of them no one would be wiser. In a few months' time she had completely emptied one of the not so petty cash accounts.

'*No worries*' she began to get creative and move funds around to cover her tracks. Even went so far as to create a dummy company and invoice the church. It was a year before the accountant uncovered the ruse and summoned her to his office.

"I'm not sure if I should call the police, tell your husband, or just pray for you," Bob Johnson sighed, labored by his choices.

The more he dug the more he realized this was embezzlement not sloppiness. Once he got the full scope he called Teresa to discuss it. Oddly enough it was Darrin who hired Bob to hide his own expenditures. The congregation didn't need to know about the house and car he purchased for Anita. The private daycare their child attended either for that matter. Everybody had secrets, especially Bob.

Anita seduced Reverend Sanders right after his wife first checked her. It was initially an act of revenge, until Darrin fell in love. Anita was a hood rat at heart and saw him as a come up. She was right, Darrin broke bread like the last supper.

When she couldn't convince him to divorce his wife she got pregnant on him. Their child's DNA was a lottery ticket. Darrin kept insisting to her he would leave Teresa and marry her but she was growing impatient.

"Don't be so dramatic!" Teresa replied nonchalantly. "I've spent a few thousand on personal needs, I fully intend to put it back!"

"A few what!" Bob gasped, "Mrs. Sanders I've uncovered over one hundred thousand dollars of theft so far! Theft Mrs. Sanders, there is no company in Atlanta by the name M.J. elevators!"

She fought the urge to smile at the clever name she thought up. M.J. elevators, cuz he got her high.

"Yeah right!" She frowned and rushed around his desk to view his monitor.

Teresa deliberately stuck her ass in his face, just in case. She could only shake her head at how amateurish her scheme appeared under scrutiny. Every coin traced directly back to her.

'I must have been high' she thought as she viewed the obvious theft for herself.

"I have to do my job. I have to tell someone, this is criminal," He said dramatically as he set snare of his own.

"Okay well you've told me. I'll handle it from here. Thank you." She said dismissing him.

"I'm afraid it doesn't work like that. This is a lot of money. You're looking at prison time," He added and paused to let it sink in. "Now, of course I can help. I can clean this up. But you'll have to help me."

Teresa heard the lust and reached for his crotch ready to suck him off at his desk to avoid going to jail.

"No! Not that!" Bob said as if repulsed. He then reached into his jacket pocket and produced a thumb drive. "This is what I like!"

"What the fuck!" Teresa spat, disgusted by the pictures on the display.

To make matters worse the accountant freed a raging hard on and began stroking it.

"It's just pictures, all I need are more pictures," He pleaded. "I'll take care of the money and pay you. Just bring me more pictures!"

It was as the images on the monitor had him possessed. Teresa watched in horror as he began to ejaculate all over himself and the desk. If she wasn't a junky she would have refused his request, but she was. So she didn't.

*****

"What are you doing?" Little Calvin asked as his mother snapped pictures of him in the tub.

At six years of age he was now uncomfortable being naked in front of his mother and on top of that his mind flashed to the photo albums in the den. He didn't want to be in them butt naked.

This is the same child who snatch his diaper off and would run naked throughout the house.

"I need you to stand back up baby," She said on the verge of tears. "It's just a game baby, help mother out."

Teresa handed over the pictures of her son in exchange for $500 and the promise to fix the books. Bob knew he had purchased her soul and intended to squeeze it dry.

The rush was on once the swap was made. Teresa rushed downtown as Bob rushed to view the pictures. He masturbated as she sped towards downtown. Teresa felt a slight panic when she dialed M.J.'s phone and finding it disconnected. She dialed repeatedly on her way just in case it got reconnected.

When that failed she drove straight to his house and came up empty. After staking the house for an hour she began doing drive-bys through the parking lots of various motels he had taken her to. That too yielded no luck. Then she headed back to his house again.

On the way she stopped to get gas, only because the incessant beep of the low-gas alert was annoying her. As soon as she pulled into the station four young goons rushed the expensive truck. Frightened at first she almost pulled off until she saw there were beating gifts.

"Dimes lady?" The quickest and first to arrive offered, proudly displaying a palm full of delicious rocks.

"Mines fatter!" Another one said appearing to be the same age as Hazel.

"I'll take them all please," Teresa beamed brightly to the delight of the drug dealing children.

She smiled at the thirty two rocks that she bought. It far exceeded the so-called "ounces" M.J. had been selling her.

"No wonder I spend so much money!" She spat realizing she'd been had.

Her mind flashed to the jewelry and fancy clothes he wore lately. The new 550, all on her dime. Well, the churches dime.

Teresa wasted a lot of time hunting dope and ignored the speed limit as she sped back to the suburbs. Despite her best efforts she still missed the arrival of the school bus.

Hazel and Calvin sat sadly on the front steps of the expensive house waiting on their mother. Not just waiting on the physical manifestation of their mother, but the warm, caring nurturer she had once been.

Before drug use turned her into Jekyll and Hyde. The worst part was that the worst part had yet to come.

Chapter 19

"I need more money. Here!" Teresa demanded as she barged into Bob's office and tossed another thumb drive on his desk. It was full of more pictures of her children including some she took of her maturing daughter while she slept. She had no idea that Bob had no use for those.

"It's not enough" he said smugly without even touching the drive or viewing the content. "I need more."

"What do you mean not enough? You haven't even looked at them. I put extra in it," She insisted.

Teresa had not smoked in days and had zero patience. She called herself quitting cold turkey but the demons finally won. Unable to use any household funds she snapped off a few hundred pictures of her children.

"Your theft was far more extensive than I thought. Honestly I'm not even sure if I will be able to cover it up. There is absolutely no way to pull any church funds for you," He lied.

Teresa frowned trying to remember just how much money she did take. The church had millions, what was he talking about.

"Look I can possibly rob Peter to pay Paul and make the problem go away and I may be able to let you borrow.... some of my own money...but like I said, I need more!" Bob was street savvy enough to know she was using. She may have been beautiful and classy but he saw through it. She was a junky. The only thing that separated her from crack whores who patrolled his Atlanta neighborhood was disposable income.

Teresa rushed around the desk preparing to kneel in front of him. If all that stood between her and getting high was a dick getting sucked then she had that problem licked. (Pun intended)

"No!" Bob shouted rolling his chair away as if he were repulsed. Picture that, a pedophile repulsed by a blow job!

"I'll give you the money you need, all I need is a little time, with him, the boy. No touching. I swear!"

"No touching!" Teresa pleaded, knowing she was going too far. She was about to drop her son off at Neverland.

******

"Now Calvin I want you to listen to Uncle Bob and behave yourself." Teresa briefed her son in the drive way of the predator's home.

"Yes mother." He replied eagerly. He was excited about the swim party and anxious to get in.

Inside Bob led Teresa to his office and produced a small lock box stuffed with cash. He made a show of counting out $1,000 and handing it over. In his mind he had just bought a little boy. It wasn't the first time.

"You said no touching!" Teresa reminded as she accepted the money. In her mind she was just renting a little boy.

"Absolutely NOT!" The child molester swore as if the notion was absurd.

He even placed his hand over his black heart for emphasis. With Hazel out with her daddy and Calvin with Uncle Bob, Teresa had rare time alone. She vowed to make the most of it. She would have loved to take her dope home to smoke in the privacy of her office. But, since Bob lived close to downtown, she opted to rent a room.

"Oh!" Teresa said sharply upon entering the motel room as various aromas assaulted her nostrils. Broken down to individual elements, she was breathing urine, semen, and vaginal secretions, blood, tobacco, weed, crack, beer, sweat and of course tears.

She rushed to open the window to let some air in and hopefully some of the funk out while she went to cop. When the luxury truck pulled into the gas station it was flocked by competing dealers. The young boys knew if she was pushing a $60,000 dollar SUV, she must be spending good.

A young hustler named Milo was first to reach her. He ducked inside the unlocked passenger side door and hit the locks to keep out his competition.

"Sup shawty wut you tryna spend?" He said in such a drawl Teresa had to process each word separately.

"How much is an ounce? A whole ounce, I have $1,000 dollars." She laid out.

"Dats how much it cost! But I don got dat much on me rat nah, so take dese, gimme da money and I'll be rat bike," he offered Ebonicly, extending five rocks.

"Well...okay" Teresa agreed trading common sense for drugs. "I'm in the motel. Room... One twenty four. You can deliver the rest of my goods there," Milo paused to look at her to see if she was serious. She was.

"Uh, ok" he agreed taking her thousand dollars for the few pebbles of crack. "I'll be rat bike!"

To her relief, the open window had dissipated some of the funk. She sat down on the bed and loaded one of the rocks onto her shooter. She lit the lighter and slowly pulled the cocaine into her life. One by one she sat and smoked the little rocks.

She periodically peaked at the window for Milo. Soon the rocks were gone, and Milo was nowhere in sight, so she decided to go look for him. "Excuse me, where's your friend!" The one with the gold teeth," she asked politely when yet another teen aged boy approached.

"Oh you da lady!" He laughed, "Shit shawty, he took that stack and gone! I got some fat dimes."

"They are indeed fat, but I have no more cash. Since you're here most days I can bring it back in the morning," She offered lusting after the large pieces of crack he showed.

Her *me time* was running short, and she needed one for the road and something for home. Lil Red stood there in silence trying to make sense of what she had said. It took a second, but he got it.

"I'll let you get three of dese for some dome," He offered.

"Dome?" Teresa questioned and looked up at the trucks dome light.

What in the world would he do with that? She wondered.

"Yeah shawty some dome, suck a nigga dick or something," he said eagerly. That she understood.

"It will cost you a lot more than three of those," she bargained.

After a brief negotiation they reached a deal of five. Teresa was slightly shocked at the size of Lil Red's dick. 'Big Red' would have been more appropriate. If this was Little Red, she would hate to meet Big Red.

"Yeah bitch suck dat dick!" he demanded as he shoved it in her face. As soon as he got inside of her mouth he grabbed her head and fucked her pretty face like crack whores in his life. Like the crack whore in her future. Like the future crack whore in her.

******

Teresa took a deep breath and exhaled loudly upon ringing Bob's door bell. A second later the smiling host opened the door.

"Mom's here!" He cheered loud enough for Calvin to hear him from the den.

"Mom!" Calvin sang happily rushing to hug his mother. "Guess what! I can swim!"

"Can you?" Teresa replied, inspecting her child with her eyes.

"Yep, Uncle Bob taught me," he replied proudly.

"Did he?" What else did you guys do?" She asked her son while looking at Bob.

"We had hot dogs, and candy and juice and...." The happy child rambled as Bob had an 'I told you so smirk on his face.'

"That's great baby", She replied while steering her child towards the door.

"Bye Calvin" Bob sang, smiling and waving.

Calvin pulled away from Teresa and ran to Uncle Bob. He jumped into his arms and embraced him.

"I love you Uncle Bob."

"I love you too," he said giving him a kiss on his cheek.

Once back at the house, Teresa was forced back into mommy mode. As usual Hazel had a million demands in addition to cooking and serving dinner. After getting the family fed and bathed, she finally got to smoke her last rock. Feeling adventurous she put the whole piece on the shooter and lit it. She was high as a satellite when she exhaled the hit.

She actually floated to bed where she planned to fuck herself. Instead, seeing that Darrin's penis had fallen out of the hole in his boxers, she eased her ass against it. She grinded herself on it and felt it stiffen. Teresa reached back and slid it into her wetness as Darrin came awake.

"Mmm Anita," he moaned and guided her flat onto her stomach. He kicked her legs wider and slid in and out of her with long even strokes.

Teresa fearfully watched the clock as the sensation began to build. She was near panic thinking he would cheat her; this close to an orgasm.

"Oh baby, fuck me!" She pleaded desperately once she was on the brink.

Darrin complied and slammed into her pounding her to the first climax of their ten year marriage.

"Argh!!!" Reverend Sanders grunted loudly as he came in his wife. "You like that?"

"Mmm loved it!" Teresa moaned, "Only thing, my name ain't no damn Anita! Get the fuck off me bastard!"

Chapter 20

"Hello Bob, I'm on the way to drop Calvin off just wanted to make sure you're home." Teresa said as she slipped into his church office.

"I sure am, come on over." He replied eagerly. She tried every possible code she should think of in attempt to break into his computer. Addresses, birth dates, phone numbers all failed. When she saw her son's name doodled inside of a heart on the desk calendar she tried "C A L V I N," mouthing as she entered her son's name.

The code gave her instant access to his computer. Knowing she didn't have time to thoroughly search the entire hard drive she copied the files to a writable DVD and logged back off.

After copying the files Teresa collected her son from the church's game room. Fueled by an overdue need to smoke one, she ignored the posted speed limits and raced downtown. She quickly accepted a thousand bucks for her kid and rushed off.

When Teresa pulled into the gas station the young thugs rushed the car. Again Milo was first to reach her. He didn't remember her and shoved an open palm full of crack rocks into the window.

"Is that all you have?" Teresa asked sweetly.

"I got plenty!" He bragged putting another pile of rocks in the window. He may not have remembered her but she damn sure remembered him.

"Hey!" Milo whined when Teresa slapped the underside of his hand sending his drugs in the air.

She got a good laugh out of the look on his face as she pulled out of the station. Since, she saved a little money. She decided to upgrade from a motel to a hotel. She ordered a nice bottle of white wine and enjoyed herself. She hated it when the time came to pick up her son. By the time she left her room, she was higher than a Jay-Z ticket.

Bob opened the door and quickly ducked his head away "Calvin!" He called averting his eyes from her causing Teresa to frown at the odd behavior.

When her son came walking shyly from the back, she wanted to cry. Little Calvin was almost limping and appeared to be in shock. A good parent would have asked 'what was wrong', but of course Teresa was a no good parent.

Besides she knew something was wrong and knew Bob was to blame. He reached out to pat the boy on his head causing Calvin to flinch and duck the contact. Teresa grabbed his hand and rushed him to the truck.

Once inside Calvin leaped the center console and embraced his mother. He hugged her so tightly she struggled to breath. It was ten minutes later when Teresa was finally able to pry her frightened child off so she could leave.

"Listen you don't have to say anything to your father. Mommy will take care of everything. You don't have to come back ok?" She pleaded.

"Ok mommy." Calvin agreed with a nod, then turned away to stare into space. Today was the first day of dealing with an issue he would have to deal with forever.

Once at home, she rushed her child into a tub of hot bubble bath. He winced from pain as he eased into the warm suds. Soon the trauma had eased away, and he began his normal bath time adventures. The small amount of blood in the boy's underwear caused her blood to boil.

Crack head or not, that is not what she sent her child over there for. She specifically said, "No Touching!" It's said that, *hell hath no fury like that of a woman scorned*, but multiply that by a mother whose child has been abused. Then stir in a volatile drug like crack and you have created a monster.

Once Teresa had put her household in order, including Reverend 'quick dick' to bed, she loaded the DVD containing Bob's files into her computer. The very first file contained enough images of naked children to put him away for life. The shots got more graphic as they went along causing Teresa to close it. She began to check the rest of the files.

"Ah-ha!" She exclaimed when she opened the financial records.

The first thing she discovered was that Bob was telling the truth about the magnitude of her theft. She could only shake her head at the one hundred thousand in phony invoices. It should have stopped there but it didn't.

"Son of a bitch!" She fumed as she counted another two hundred grand Bob had stolen that would be linked directly to her. "Oh I got you, you dirty mother-fucker. I got you!"

She skipped the file labeled 'pastor' in favor of sneaking out of the garage and hitting the few rocks she had left over. A variety of vengeful plots circulated in her convoluted mind, as the crack swirled through her being.

Teresa finally settled on murder. She was going to have him killed and let him take blame for all of the missing money. On her next foray into Atlanta's underbelly, Teresa ordered a pistol to go along with her crack. She was surprised at how easy it was to find one. When she informed the dealer who served her that she had five hundred dollars to spend, he quickly pulled one out of his waistband and tossed it onto her seat.

The 380 caliber pistol looked new but had already changed hands in the hood several times. It had an active role in two homicides and a handful of armed robberies. It should have been tossed in a sewer months ago, but five hundred dollars was better. Especially since the cheap gun cost eighty nine bucks new.

The sale of the gun plus the eight ball of dope Teresa bought, meant the dealer could close shop early. It was time to hit the mall for an outfit for the teen club later and ball out.

"That's that bitch dat stole my bomb," Milo growled to the dealer who just completed the sale. "I'm finna go rob her ass, should murk her."

"Go 'head, 'cept she strapped. I just sold her a burner," He cautioned.

Milo, while dumb, was not that dumb. He would not confront an armed woman. He'd have to catch her later.

Once Teresa got inside her motel room she wasted no time. She chipped off a cardiac arrest size piece of crack and loaded it onto her shooter. The blast was so strong she actually looked down to make sure she hadn't levitated.

The blast made her so horny that it soaked her panties. She stripped off every stitch of clothing and began to touch herself. In this heightened state it only took seconds for her to climax. The strong orgasm seemed to shake the room for several seconds. While it did offer some relief ultimately she was unfulfilled. She wanted to be filled.

"I know what I'm about to do!" She huffed as she got dressed again. She took a hit from the remnants left in the shooter and set out.

Teresa scanned every man she saw from head to toe, in search of 'Mr. Right Now'. She was looking for a nice, sturdy young man to rock her world. That's exactly what she found.

"Excuse me" she smiled stopping a construction worked in mid stride.

Judging by his six foot five iron worker's frame he had to be working with something.

"Sup Miss?" He replied politely, displaying both interest and impatience.

"Do you have an hour or so you can spare? To help a lady in despair," she asked helplessly.

"Umm...I'm on break. I only got twenty minutes," he said looking at his watch.

"That will have to do!" Teresa exclaimed grabbing his wrist and leading him away.

The lucky man was stunned at how quickly she peeled off her clothes once they reached the room.

"Time's wasting young man," She warned.

He dropped his dingy jeans to his ankles and waddled over to the bed where Teresa awaited on hands and knees. It was a short walk but he had a raging hard on when he arrived.

Teresa came every few strokes of his long penis when his knees buckled from his own orgasm, she was thoroughly satisfied, and, with two minutes left to spare.

Chapter 21

"Bob Johnson" the child molester sang cheerfully as he answered his line.

He didn't recognize the number and hoped it was in response to the ad he'd run for piano lessons.

"Hey Bob this is Teresa, Calvin's mom." Teresa said forcing herself to sound pleasant. "I'll be in the area later and Calvin is absolutely begging to come see you!"

"He is?" Bob asked bewildered. He remembered how much of a fight the little boy put up. "He said that?"

"Begging! I don't know what you did to my son, but he loves his Uncle Bob! What did you do to my son?" Teresa said struggling to maintain her composure.

"Me... umm, well just you know, boy stuff," Bob stammered. He fought an erection and lost at the thought of the precious boy coming back.

"Okay, so we'll pop through in a few then." She sang and closed the pre-paid phone purchased for the mission.

She thought about the eight ball of crack she had and almost aborted the mission. Teresa drove her rental car past the house several times trying to summon the courage for the task at hand. She couldn't.

In the end she decided to just go smoke. She did a U-Turn prepared to leave but as she neared his home she got angry. The memory of the horrified look on her son's face caused her to whip into his driveway.

She was in full momma grizzly bear mode when she rang the bell. The bloody briefs popped into her mind as he unlocked the door.

While smiling, Bob pulled open his front door. Teresa promptly shot him in his face. He tried to say something, but the bullet tearing through his cheek and destroying his jaw made him forget what he was saying. It is hard to concentrate with hot lead ripping through flesh and bones. It has a way of making one lose one's train of thought.

Since he was unable to get his point across Bob turned and ran. Teresa closed the door behind him and followed him shooting at his back. All six rounds found their mark and all six were fatal in their own right, however none caused instant death.

Now, Bob would have to suffer his last moments above the ground. He would just have to deal with the shredded organs and ripped arteries, the torn flesh and broken bones.

Have to accept the shortness of breath from punctured lungs and grow cold from blood loss. Teresa would have loved to take a seat and watch him expire, but she had to work to do. She rushed to his office and logged into his system. It only took a few minutes to transfer all guilt of the embezzlement back to Bob. She painfully deleted her children's pictures from the thousands he had on file.

Some showing what he actually did to kids, those she left. Next the financials files marked 'Pastor' were copied to a thumb drive, before they too were deleted. Finally, a 'wiper' program removed all traces of her work.

A smile spread across Teresa's pretty face as she completely emptied the cash box. Bob had taken one last ragged breath as she neared but didn't live long enough to exhale it. Teresa stepped over his body like he was no more than a puddle. Once she got to her hotel room, she spread the twenty grand from the safe onto the bed and got high.

*****

The bad news of Bob's early departure travelled quickly. By the time Teresa made it home she began fielding calls from nosey members of the congregation. Everyone wanted to be first to spread the bad news.

Once she told, 'sister spread the word' and 'brother got the scoop' that she was already informed, they quickly hung up to further water the grape vine.

Darrin was near panic but was more concerned with Bob's computer than his life. Whatever was on the system sent him racing to the church to retrieve his C.P.U. Once he got it home he frantically tried to log in.

"Dear," Teresa began, then paused from the bitter taste that the phony term of endearment left on her tongue. She just realized she hated the man.

"You know, I can help you with whatever it is you're trying to do." She offered as he struggled to get in.

"No!!!" He yelled so urgently that it startled her. It also made her more curious as to what he was searching for. Teresa rushed upstairs to her office and loaded the thumb drive.

The file labeled "Pastor" had sub-files, so she went straight to the financial records. The first thing she noticed was that there were two sets of books. One for the benefit of church supporters and the IRS, the other told the truth.

The truth was that ole Rev had two households. According to the records her husband owned a half a million dollar house a few miles away from the one they shared. She began matching up the records to the facts.

There were daycare receipts for two small children, Anita had two small children. A new Lexus, Anita had a new Lexus, clothes, trips, cash; in all, he was spending there rather than here. He spent nights here but spent his dough there.

Teresa was able to match up some of the expenditures with the lies that went along with them. That so-called minister's retreat in Cancun, the jewelry, everything traced back to Anita. To add fuel to the already blazing fire the next file contained pictures of Darrin, Anita and their two big headed ugly children.

Teresa ridiculed shot after shot, amusing herself by talking trash about the couple. The next file wasn't so funny. In it contained DNA reports that Bob had run. It showed that Calvin was not Darrin's, but neither was his son with Anita, Darrin Jr. Obviously Anita had been creeping as well.

Last but not least was Reverend Darrin Sanders's will. It equally divided his small fortune between his two families. Anita would receive the same amount as she, his wife of so many years, if or when Darrin died.

Teresa decided right then that he was gonna die a lot sooner than he thought. And his tramp baby momma secretary wasn't going to see a dime. Ask any killer and they'll tell you that subsequent murders are easier than first.

"Any luck honey?" Teresa asked so sweetly. Darrin looked around puzzled.

He knew there was not a trace of affection in his wife's heart for him. The feeling was mutual. He only stayed to keep up appearances. How could he counsel others if his own house wasn't in order?

Of course Anita was livid and making demands and ultimatums. When she got too fussy, he took her on a trip or bought her a gift.

"No, I'll still have a tech come tomorrow." He said, standing to leave. "Don't touch it while I'm gone."

"Okay," she sang in a submissive tone, that made her and her husband frown. He knew the bitch didn't have a submissive bone in her body.

His car wasn't even out of the driveway before Teresa logged onto the system. It only took a few minutes to change the will, removing all traces of his concubine. Now she wasn't getting shit.

The pictures and DNA reports were replaced with a blackmail letter from Bob demanding 500 grand not to release the second set of books. After a quick sweep of the system with her 'wiper' program, she made the call.

"Atlanta police, how can I help you?" The dispatcher asked when she came on the line.

"Yes, I'm a co-worker of Bob Johnson. He works at our church. He was killed today and we have his computer. We wanted to turn it in just in case it can help you in your investigation." Teresa said fighting not to laugh.

"We'll send someone right over."

Chapter 22

Darrin was superheated about Teresa turning the computer over to the authorities before he got a chance to look in it. He didn't speak to her for days afterwards. Luckily for him the police stored the computer in the evidence room and never looked at it. Without a tip or reason to investigate, it was ignored. That's why she felt his next move was an act of revenge. It was about to blow up in her face.

"Teresa we need to talk," he began as she entered his office. She plopped down in the chair and glared at him.

"Well talk!" She spat stopping just short of calling him a name. She was already hot about having been 'summoned' to his office in the first place. Then to be told to 'wait' and 'Pastor will see you now' by his bitch added insult to injury.

"I want to talk to you about forgiveness," he began. He was using his pulpit voice and was about to piss her off. "We expect, ask, beg even for all-mighty God to forgive us, and yet won't forgive each other. We recite the Lord's Prayer asking for him to forgive us our trespasses but don't forgive those who trespass against us."

"Darrin I forgive." Teresa smiled through the tears streaming down her face.

She assumed he was apologizing in an attempt at reconciliation. If her husband would forgive her she would certainly forgive him. That's just what she needed, she was getting out of control and she knew it.

"I'm glad to hear that Teresa, here." He smiled handing a document across the desk to her.

"Fuck is this!" She barked halfway down the page. "Are you fucking serious! After what he did to me!"

"Sit your ass back down, and shut up!" He demanded rising to his feet.

Darrin had never taken that tone with her, and it worked. She sat her ass back down and shut up. If he had he done that from day one, this would have been a short story.

"You have two choices. You either sign the paper or quit working here." He said plainly. "The man is up for parole, he needs a job. Considering the uncertainty surrounding the situation I...."

"The what?" Teresa whined. Over the years she forgot that she wasn't really a victim. You live a lie for so long it becomes a truth.

"Fine, I'll sign the damn paper!" She did and tossed it at her husband, stormed out.

As she passed his smirking mistress, she thought it might not be so bad to see ole big dick Edwin again. By the time she reached her own office a plan was hatched.

****

Anytime Teresa got stressed she got high. Having to sign a release allowing her "rapist" a job stressed her to the gills. Actually any excuse would do and off she went to get high.

As was her habit she rented a room then set out in search of dope. Another habit she had was dialing M.J.'s old numbers. His cell number had long been reassigned and whoever answered the house phone always said. "He ain't hure!"

"Yeah" a gravelly voice growled upon answering.

"M.J.?" Teresa asked at the sound of the foreign yet familiar voice.

"Dis me, who dis?" He answered and asked.

"This is your teacher." Teresa purred seductively.

"Sho-nuff! Where you at shawty?" He asked eagerly.

She gave him the name of the hotel and room number then prepared for his visit. That preparation consisted of a large hit and a quick shower.

Looking to surprise him she neglected to get dressed. Instead she wrapped in the plush towel and let wet hair frame her face. It was Teresa who was in for the surprise when she opened the door and a skinny, disheveled M.J. smiled minus a front tooth.

"Sup shawty." The hull of the former hunk asked, as he walked in. "You got some mo of dat?"

He said sniffing the remnants of crack in the air. The shooter and rocks laying on the tabled answered for the shocked woman, and he took off toward it.

"I'm fine, thanks for asking. And you?" Teresa quipped to his back as he rushed the dope.

M.J. heard her but didn't answer until he blew the huge hit, filling the room with smoke.

"Shit shawty, shit been crazy!" Got locked up, got out. Got locked back up again. I'm cool now though," He said fixing himself yet another hit.

"Well, I've missed....you." Teresa said thinking about his dick. He looked a mess but she was hoping he could still fuck.

He couldn't. M.J. did lick and suck her lonely vagina until she couldn't take it anymore. But when he stood up his dick dangled harmlessly between his legs.

"Huh?" Teresa asked wearing a confused frown.

"Shit shawty I done smoked way too much blow for a nigga dick to get hard!" He proclaimed almost proudly.

Not wanting to be out-smoked she joined him at the table. Luckily for her she had only laid out a portion of the drugs because M.J. was smoking everything in sight.

On the drive home Teresa stopped just short of deleting his number from her phone. In the end she decided that a crack-head on staff could come in handy. Somebody had to do the dirty work.

Chapter 23

"You know, you can't keep ducking me every time you see me. Eventually we'll have to talk," Edwin said running into Teresa in the church's copy room.

"Talk?! Fuck we got to talk about!" She demanded.

In the couple of months that he had been working there, she ran every time she saw him.

"Rape? You want to talk about you raping me?" She complained.

"I am a different person than I was. I deserve everything that I got," He offered contritely. "I'm sorry."

The apology had instantly softened her heart. Not to mention he was fine. They say prison preserves a person. It had certainly been kind to him during the fifteen years. And while it did change him, being free was changing him back.

The free world offered more temptation than he could stand. Even the good church ladies were pushing pussy at the eligible bachelor. It was just a matter of time. He was bound to hit something.

"I accept, but let's just keep our distance. We can co-exist in the same place." Teresa said calmly.

She walked off and put a little something extra in her hips for his benefit. He appreciated it too as he watched her hips sway down the hallway.

With the money Teresa got from the dearly departed accountant she had the resources to lead a double life. Every day she would get her children off to school then head over to the church. She would put in a couple of hours in her office before heading downtown. An advance call to Lil Red meant the dope would be waiting for her at the hotel. She would smoke for a few hours and then back to the office, then home.

That was her routine during the week, but weekends were more challenging. Hazel was old enough now to take care of herself and her brother, but Darrin forbid them being home alone. He also refused to stay home with them while she ran errands. That's why the poor kids were enrolled in ballet, soccer, baseball, basketball, swimming, and music lessons.

Teresa dropped them off at whatever was on their schedule and rushed to get high. Occasionally, Teresa would drive by the house Darrin shared with his other family.

She was only able to tolerate it because of her own activities. Everyone has secrets. It wasn't until she passed and saw that Darrin and Anita were having a BB&Q and pool party that she got pissed. The fact that he was flaunting his other family. Oh he had to go!

Knowing Reverend Edwin would be her soon dead husband's replacement, she decided to get next to him. She would still be the First Lady.

Edwin was well liked and had shined every time Darrin gave him the pulpit. Likewise, the drop dead gorgeous, yet mysterious, Reverend Cash was a close runner up. He had dark piercing eyes set deeply within his handsome chestnut face. 'Good' hair and the body of a professional point guard.

Teresa would have preferred him, but he was so elusive. All she could get out of the man was a flash of his dazzling smile to accompany a 'morning', 'evening' or 'afternoon'.

Yes, Reverend William Cash aka Dollar Bill was another story, another story for another time.

Besides she had leverage on Edwin. He had no choice but to cooperate. It was either that or back to prison.

"Hello? Umm excuse me," Teresa smiled politely as she stuck her head in Edwin's office. "I didn't think anyone else was here."

"Umm.. I'm the only one left I believe. Everyone else is over at Calvary Baptist for the Reverend Butt's retirement party." Edwin replied.

"Just you and I, alone. Interesting." She said seductively as she eased in the door behind her.

"Mrs. Sanders I... I'm not comfortable being alone in a room with you," he said with fear audible in his voice.

"Nigga you wasn't scared to put your dick in my mouth while I was unconscious. Oh I read the police report." She laughed wickedly. "I lied on you then and I'll do it again"

"What do you want from me?" He whined.

"Everything!" She spat, "but first I'll take some sex and it better be good."

Even though Edwin was scared, loyal, and on parole, when Teresa dropped her dress his dick responded to her thickness. She sat spread eagle on his desk and leaned back. One doesn't need to RSVP to eat some pussy, so he dove right in.

Being as backed up as she was the Preacher's Wife came in seconds. Proud of his fancy tongue-man-ship Edwin stood up with a wet smile. He whipped out his impressive erection and rushed inside while she was still quivering. He slammed in and out of her so hard it was obvious he intended to punish her. Teresa loved it. She squealed from a second orgasm seconds before he pulled out and exploded into his handkerchief.

"I read the police report too." He said breathlessly.

Her vagina full of his cum is what prevented him from fighting the case years back. He was urged by his lawyer to plead out to twenty years and avoid a life sentence.

"So what now?" Edwin asked meaning he wanted more.

"My husband is on the way out," she said frankly. "You can go with him or stay with me. Either way I'll always be First Lady."

Edwin was a friend to himself first and foremost. He knew being at the helm of the mega-church meant millions. And if the beautiful woman who just knelt in front of him and took half of him into her mouth was part of the deal, then so be it.

Teresa was all smiles as she floated out of Edwin's office. Not only did she get her boots knocked properly but had secured an ally.

Reverend Cash was coming out of his office at the same time, but ducked back in when he saw him.

"What! Is it the Pastor?" Teresa asked fearfully.

"Just a janitor" he lied. "Let's give him a few minutes before we leave."

Of course he used those few minutes to sex her one more time. He had his eyes on the prize too, and when he found out Rev had a girlfriend he moved on her.

Anita was too young and naive to realize she was a pawn in a complex game of chess. He had convinced her that Reverend Sanders was using her. That he had no plans on divorcing his wife. Now that he had seduced her it was time to make his own play for the throne.

Check!

Chapter 24

Teresa pulled M.J.'s bitter tasting sweaty dick out of her mouth to explain his task one more time. She realized he smoked a great deal of brain cells.

"How would you like this every day?" she purred between licks. M.J. shot a glance to the rock on the table and replied in the affirmative.

He could care less about some head, or pussy, or food for that matter. He wanted to get high. His dabbling with coke finally caught up with him as it does a lot of dealers.

Somehow they seem to forget rule number four: 'Never get high on your own supply!'

He fought the good fight, but eventually fell victim to the pipe. How ironic is it that the same woman he introduced the crack to was now controlling him with it. Even the few prison bids he served didn't quell his thirst for dope. It only hibernated until the very day he got released, then demanded to be fed.

When he first began smoking crack daily he was still moving enough product to smoke for free. The scales gradually tipped until he was a full-fledged junky. He smoked away all of his earthly possessions.

Now he stole, begged and borrowed to get high. Occasionally his former teacher would scoop him up and get him high for sex. He had a couple guys who did the same for him.

She finally managed to get an erection out of him and quickly mounted it. She rode him hard and fast until she climaxed. The couple then moved over to the table to smoke.

"You know we can get as much dope as we want if we get this money," she urged. "What money?" he asked as if she hadn't already explained twice.

"I already told you," she sang girlishly. Fact was, she hated to have to repeat the death penalty worthy statement.

"My husband has a million dollars." she threw out.

"Shit, where he keep it? I'll go steal it." He said like it was just that simple. Perhaps he had the million in his wallet and he could just go pick his pocket.

"You can't steal it silly! It's in his will. They will give me the money once he dies." She said still singing and dancing around.

"So when dat nigga finna die?"

"As soon as you kill him. I want you to kill my husband," she finally stated plainly.

"OK. When?" He replied as if she had asked him to wash her car.

"This weekend, my kids will be at my dad's. Here's the plan ...."

******

"Cornish hen stuffed with wild rice and mushrooms," Teresa announced sitting the plate in front of her skeptical husband. It wasn't just the elaborate meal; she was using the 'good China' to boot.

"Why are you being so nice to me all of a sudden," Darrin asked bluntly.

He was done, over, wanted a divorce. The only reason he even agreed to dinner was to break the news. Half of the congregation was divorced. They would get over it.

Then he could announce his plans to marry the beloved church secretary who was struggling to take care of her children all by herself. Anita had been pulling away lately, becoming more distant by the day. He could only assume it was because he had yet to marry her like he'd been promising for years. He had assumed wrong.

Fact was Reverend Cash put that dick on her and everything changed. Dollar Bill's dick game was ridiculous. The only thing that surpassed it was his smooth talk. Rev could have been a pimp in another life. Actually he was, but again, that's another story. Literally.

'Because it's your last meal, you sorry son of bitch' Teresa mused to herself as the thought crossed her mind. She let that one pass silently and went with the next one.

"Because you're my husband. You deserve it and I love you." she managed without choking.

That threw the Reverend for a loop. He did not expect to hear that. Never in a thousand years would he think the woman still loved him. He had run out of love for her a long time ago.

If he had been totally honest to himself, he would have to admit the only reason he asked her to marry him was to appear noble in front of her father. It worked to because Darrin benefitted greatly by being related to the great man.

That was then, this is now. His own name and congregations were big enough to take the hit of a divorce. If his wife put up any resistance the pictures of her buying drugs and checking into hotels with men would surface.

"Well the only way to say this is to just come on out and say it. Teresa I want a divorce," Darrin said plainly.

"Ok, that's fine. Pretty sure Anita has waited long enough," Teresa replied, "Cute kids you guys have."

"You know?" He replied shocked. He swore he covered his tracks better than that. "Well, I know about your indiscretions as well."

Teresa stifled a laugh thinking *which ones?* Instead, she set her plan in motion.

"No need for any threats, we can do this in a civil manner. I only have one request from you. And I will not take no for an answer,"

"What is it?" Darrin demanded.

"Make love to me one last time" she pleaded.

She loathed having the man inside of her, but it was part of the plan. Her vagina would be the spider web, and a dingy spider was lurking nearby. "It's the least you could do."

Darrin was actually shocked how good the sex was. With the burden of the loveless marriage lifted he enjoyed every slow stroke. Teresa was face down, ass up. And he loved it.

Sex with Anita had changed. Even her vagina seemed different. If he didn't know any better he would have sworn Anita was seeing someone, someone with a rather large penis.

She was, Reverend Cash. His dick was urban fiction big. Ten inches long, thick as a baby's leg with a big ole mushroom shaped head. He was literally rearranging her pussy, moving walls back and knocking the bottom out of it.

"I see you like it huh? You know you gonna miss this good pussy huh?" Teresa tensed, squeezed his shaft with her vaginal muscle.

Reverend Sanders opened his mouth to reply but the room lit up twice from the 22 Caliber pistol. M.J. fired into the back of his head.

"Shit! You could have given him a few more minutes! He almost made me cum." Teresa complained.

"I got you." M.J. said stepping forward.

He had gotten an erection from watching the couple have sex. He whipped it out and shoved himself inside, standing right over the dead preacher. The unholy couple fucked as the Reverend's blood soaked the carpet. No worries, she planned to change it with the insurance money anyway.

M.J. took Teresa over the edge then joined her with his own orgasm. He grunted and filled her vagina with recently infected semen. He now killed two people tonight. Luckily, he wouldn't have to go to jail for either murder.

"Tell me you have something," Teresa pleaded, the second she recovered from her orgasm.

"Yeah, I brung a couple sacks" he replied reaching for his dirty jeans.

M.J. retrieved his well-used straight shooter and a few small bags of dope.

The two of them chit chatted over hits of crack right next to the dead body. Teresa monitored the crack supply and when it reached a critical low it was time to implement part two of her plan.

"Babe, grab my purse. I got a few sacks in my purse" Teresa sang sweetly, rubbing his back. When he bent over to comply with the request she bent too.

"In here?" He questioned as he fished around in the purse putting his well-known finger prints on everything.

For a reply, Teresa stood over him and fired the four remaining rounds into his back. None of the bullets were instantly fatal, meaning it would be a slow painful death.

To make matters worse for M.J. he had to sit there and watch his killer smoke his dope before he died. The tattered lungs meant he couldn't speak as he just looked on lustfully.

"Really? Are you kidding me?" Teresa laughed upon seeing his dilemma. In an act of twisted mercy she took a hearty pull and blew the smoke into his mouth. M.J. breathed in his final blast but did not exhale. He took it to hell with him.

With that final blast M.J. gave up and let go. The death rattle from his throat as his soul left his body alerted Teresa that she was alone in the room. She picked up the phone and dialed.

"9-1-1 what's your emergency?" the dispatcher asked devoid of the slightest trace of concern.

"A man just broke into our home, he killed my husband and sexually assaulted me" Teresa reported. She was so calm the dispatcher wasn't sure if she had heard her correctly.

"Ma'am did, you say someone killed your husband?" she repeated. "Is the attacker still there?"

"Yes and yes" Teresa said curtly. "The man killed my husband. He is still here. I killed him."

"Police and rescue are on the way!" the dispatcher urged, "please stay on the line."

The plan to make it look like a burglary worked like a charm since M.J. pried open the back door and left his well-documented finger prints everywhere. The rape kit confirmed her story of sexual assault and the case was closed, for now.

Chapter 25

The sudden death of the beloved preacher shocked the congregation to its collective core. Meetings and sub-meetings were held to see who would now run the show. It came down to Reverend Cash and the pastor's close friend Edwin. It was Edwin's close relationship that gave him the edge. A final meeting was called to finalize the selection.

"Rev, can I get a quick second before the meeting starts?" Reverend Cash asked into the intercom system.

"I don't think we have time." Edwin replied dismissively. He was eager to get to the meeting where he would be anointed the head nigga in charge'.

"Eddie, I assure you that one, it's of extreme importance. And two, it effects what is about to happen. Besides you have to pass by my office anyway." Cash said with a smile you could hear over the phone.

Edwin fought the urge to chump him off. He wasn't particularly fond of the flamboyant fly guy preacher. He couldn't wait for him to be working for him.

'*Might fire his ass,*' Edwin mused as he walked down the hall.

"Make this quick!" Edwin demanded, barging into Reverend Cash's office without knocking. That was designed to get him used to being an underling.

Cash just laughed, knowing what was coming. He lifted the remote and pressed 'play'. Edwin frowned when he appeared on the screen at his desk.

"I did the editing by myself" Cash chuckled smugly. "Not bad for a novice."

"We don't have much time, the sermon just started," Teresa exclaimed as she rushed into the scene.

"I'm ready!" The Edwin on the TV proclaimed as he stood up and revealed his erection, as the real life Edwin grimaced.

It was obvious that more than one camera was used when the angle switched just as Teresa knelt in front of him and granted access to the back of her throat. After a few minutes of oral sex, that had both men hard, the preacher's wife bent over her husband's best friend's desk.

The cameras switched again just as Edwin pulled her dress up and rammed into her. He was fucking her so hard; the sound of skin slapping could clearly be heard. The angle was great, clearly showing their 'fuck faces' as they cursed and fucked. While service was going on no less.

"I'm gonna need you to decline the position and recommend me." Cash explained, over the film, Eddie announcing he was cuming.

"What's to stop me from taking this disk and telling you to fuck yourself?" Edwin demanded desperately.

He sized Reverend Cash up and thought he could take him if it came to that. They were both the same height and built but Edwin had been in prison and thought that would give him the edge. Only Cash had been to jail too, just no one knew it.

"One, you can have the disk! It's your copy," he replied, putting emphasis on the word copy letting him know it was just that. "And two, If you ever! Try me I will kill you. Make no mistake about it!"

"Well you know my co-star has a tremendous say in the matter," Edwin croaked. Teresa was his ace in the hole, or so he thought.

"Did you forget she's on the tape too?" Cash laughed. "Besides," he added handing him a yellow envelope.

"What is this?" the beaten man asked fearfully.

"Open and see," Cash laughed.

"The fuck?!" Edwin exclaimed as he thumbed through the stack of pictures. "This is that guy!"

M.J.'s picture had been on all the news channels as the killer of the prominent pastor. Pictures of him and Teresa together caused his knees to buckle forcing him to sit.

"She was down with that shit?" He asked still sorting through the pictures. Her statement about his being on the way out flashed in his mind.

"Mrs. Sanders will be arrested as soon as she shows up," Cash assured.

He knew since he supplied the police with the pictures himself. He had to move quick before the insurance paid out.

"Now the insurance will come to the church, to us". Cash beamed.

Reverend Cash didn't bother about telling him that half would go to Anita. Of course he didn't know that Teresa had already burned the bridge.

Cash had to fight an erection at the prospect of all the money. He could get a lot of pussy with all that money. A lot of his other vices as well, and he had some expensive vices.

"I guess we can split the money," Edwin offered accepting the offer.

"Split no, but I will break bread. You won't be doing any worse than you're doing now" Cash assured him.

There were stunned faces and a little murmuring when Edwin declined the position and offered Reverend in his place. It didn't take much for the deacons and trustees to be persuaded that he was better suited for the job. And of course, he would be at his side the whole way. Or so he thought.

The plan to expose Mrs. Sanders right before she was carted off to jail fell through when she didn't show up for the meeting. The non-suspecting board eagerly excused her since she had taken her husband's death so hard. She hadn't been seen since the murder.

It was a good thing that Hazel was old enough and matured enough to take care of herself and her brother; because Teresa was a no-show at home as well. With a one point two million insurance payout on the horizon Teresa intend to burn through all the available cash on hand. Since Darrin wasn't around to look over her shoulder, she was reckless.

She got herself a room downtown and summoned 'Lil Red' to bring her blow. On a few occasions she allowed the little man with the big dick to explore her vagina.

Teresa so rarely even checked in at home, she had no idea when her world began to crash. It took a trip to the ATM to discover she had a problem.

Chapter 26

"I'll take the max please," Teresa smiled to her rapidly changing reflection in the ATM's camera.

"What the fuck!" Teresa pressed buttons in rapid succession after the machine ate her card. When nothing worked she fished out another card and yet another when the machine kept those as well.

As directed the ATM snapped pictures of the wanted woman and notified police. Teresa was totally unaware when she stormed into the branch. She bypassed the line and approached a teller. The rude move would have gotten a few stern glances in her upscale part of town, but she was now in the hood.

"Oh hell naw!" the woman who would have been next screamed, as Teresa laid her ID on the counter.

"Just one minute," Teresa demanded as if her business was more important.

"One minute my ass," the hood rat said approaching. As Teresa and the ghetto diva argued the teller glanced at the familiar name on the driver's license. It was the same name on an alert issued that morning. She waved the sleepy security guard over.

The lazy man sighed at the interruption and grudgingly came over. He passed right by the women as they escalated their argument to a shoving match.

"She has a warrant! Hold her while I call the police," the teller announced loud enough to be heard by combatants.

The ghetto girl, named Chic-Falia, after her mom's favorite food, assumed they meant her and tore out of there with her fake ID and forged check. The chubby guard followed her but only with his eyes.

"Not her, her!" the teller shouted again pointing to Teresa. "Grab her!"

"I don't get paid to grab people," the human scare crow replied nonchalantly.

123

He was right too, his job was too sit there. For eight bucks an hour, what more could you expect out of him?

Teresa was frazzled when she made it back to her hotel room. For the first time in days her children came to her mind. She rushed into her purse to call her kids but ... there was her pipe.

She hadn't had a hit all day and after the incident at the bank, she felt she really needed one. Deserved one, for all she'd been through. There were no rocks left, but the accumulation of residue left over from weeks of heavy smoking looked absolutely scrumptious. She dropped the phone and picked up her pipe.

The late M.J. was the one who use to 'push' the shooter to smoke the remains. Teresa mimicked what she had seen him do on numerous occasions and got a nice healthy blast.

Elation filled her convoluted mind as the deadly smoke filled her lungs. She held the precious smoke as one would hold onto their last breath. The 'leftovers' in the pipe afforded her several more hits before it ran dry. It was then that she remembered her children again.

"Hazel baby?" Teresa asked sweetly as her abandoned daughter's cell phoned was answered.

"Mom?" she replied with a frown that could be heard over the line.

"Yes, it's me baby, I'm sorry. I..."

"Mrs. Sanders?" a strange voice asked coming on the line.

"Who is this? Put my child back on the line!" Teresa demanded hotly.

"Ma'am my name is Lisa Jones. I'm with child protective services. Your children have been placed in state custody pending a hearing. We need you ..."

"Who! A what? Bitch I don't have time to play with you. Put 'my' child back on the phone that 'I' bought for her!"

"Bitch did you say?" Ms. Jones laughed. She looked around to make sure the children were out of ear-shot before responding.

"Bitch your kids have been in state custody for over a day. And that's after being home alone for days before that! Oh, let's not forget the police warrant for your arrest for killing your husband! A preacher!" Ms. Jones spat, "But I'm a Bitch? Bitch, please!"

The words caused the phone to fall out of her hands. Teresa scrambled to hang up the phone so she wouldn't have to hear anymore.

'How? Why?' she wondered, trying to figure out what had happened.

How was she now implicated, it went off without a hitch. Former student breaks into the house, kills her husband, then, rapes her. She killed the attacker in self-defense. Case closed.

'And what about my money? How am I supposed to get high!' Teresa whined thinking about what was really important.

"Voila!" she cheered as her emergency prepaid credit cards came to mind.

Her phone rang as she left the room but she ignored the private call. Police were still able to trace what tower she was near and dispatcher units to apprehend the double murder suspect. They missed her by a few minutes.

Teresa took out fifteen hundred, the limit, which amounted to half of the balance on the card. Two hundred went for rent on an extended stay motel. 'Lil Red' got most of the rest of it. Fortunately for Teresa it took him a few hours to come by, and she used that anxious time at a nearby Dollar Store and Burger joint.

Teresa amused herself at the cheap items she needed for her new life. She wouldn't need as much as there wasn't much life left for her.

The first fifteen hundred lasted just over a week of heavy smoking. When she withdrew the last of the cash common sense urged her to be frugal, but she had broken ties with common sense a while ago.

She did begin socializing with some of the other junkies who frequented the hotel. Most turned tricks to support their habits.

A prospect that the still sidity crack head scoffed at. She had options, she would not be trading herself for dope, or so she thought.

Chapter 27

"What now?" Teresa asked herself as she exhaled the last of the residue from her pipe. She hadn't realized she said it aloud until her two companions answered.

"Just suck some dick!" Sherry cheered.

"Yeah, it's easy and fun!" Tracy eagerly co-signed. "Most of life's problems can be solved with a blow job!"

"So, you're telling me ... that all that stands between world-peace is somebody getting their dick sucked?" Teresa laughed, "The whole Middle East thing? Dafur?"

"Mm hmm!" both crack heads nodded happily.

"Wall street? Bloods and Crips? Tom and Jerry?" Teresa teased.

"Yup, Yup, and Yup," they replied.

She was getting a kick out of her new friends, but she was not turning tricks with strange men.

She knew sex for money was in her immediate future but she didn't know with who. Her boyfriend Edwin should be firmly in charge of the church by now, he surely could help her with her legal issues. If not, at least give her some money to get high.

"Teresa?" Edwin asked when she came on the line. "Where are you? Everyone is looking for you!"

"Mmm, you too?" Teresa purred seductively ignoring the obvious. She watched the news and knew she was wanted.

Good thing for Teresa, was that she was securely in the underbelly of society. A place where no one gave a fuck about anything or anyone, except getting high. A place where both dealers and users alike traded their dignity, morals, lives, and souls for their desires.

Desires were God here, and they had their own commandments. But this false God had no mercy. Like all false Gods had no power.

"Uh ... yeah, me too," Edwin lied. The sexy tone of her voice enticed him to tap that ass one last time, but he quickly shook it off. She was the only threat to him and his own goals.

"I'm at the Akorn Lodge on Memorial, bring me some money. A few thousand should hold me until I can clear up this whole business," Teresa explained.

"Uh ... sure, Akorn Lodge, I'm on the way," he lied again. Instead of going himself, he sent the police.

Luck was either for or against Teresa, because she just happened to be at the store across the street when the fugitive squad converged on the seedy motel. When a light is cut on, crack-heads scurry for cover like roaches. Most had wants and warrants, and they made themselves scarce.

"Edwin!" she fumed as the police made a bee-line to her room and knocked the door off its hinges. It didn't take a rocket scientist to know he put the cops oh her. "You're a dead man!"

She could only watch as her two companions were carted off to jail. Both Sherry and Tracy had outstanding warrants for crack related offenses. Not to mention the pipes and drugs found in the room. A single tear escaped her eye as police searched, then impounded her vehicle.

Teresa was now alone and on foot in the mean streets of Atlanta. Nothing in her sheltered life prepared her for what was ahead. These streets consumed even the hardest of souls. Teresa, it would swallow whole.

Once the police spread out with her picture to canvas the area, the show was over. Teresa blended in with the crowd and fled the area. It didn't take long to get picked up since the pretty woman stood out from the usual crack whore selection.

"How much for head and fuck?" The driver asked once Teresa was seated.

"Five hundred," She stated plainly and almost got whiplash from him slamming on the brakes.

"Shit shawty a nigga can get straight for twenty bucks or a couple sacks round here!" He protested.

Teresa heard the word sack and held her spot. She had only run across the street to fetch a new lighter to smoke what her friends had sucked out of their customers. Then again she hadn't eaten yet and was quite hungry. Twenty dollars, while paltry would certainly take care of her immediate problems. Ten for a decent meal and ten on some dope sounded about right.

"Tell you what young man," Teresa began, sounding like Mrs. Sanders the teacher. "I will take you up on your offer of twenty bucks!"

"That's what's up" the young trick said and pulled back into traffic. A few turns later he pulled into the lot of yet another run-down motel.

Instead of a room he pulled around back and pulled out his semi erection. Teresa had a flash of shame but he desires outweighed it and down she went. When her customer's body language screamed *'I'm cuming'* she pulled him out of her mouth as he began to ejaculate.

"Fuck you doing shawty?" he fumed as his designer jeans became covered in semen.

"You didn't honestly expect me to allow you to ejaculate in my mouth! For twenty dollars!" Teresa frowned.

"Bitch get out my damn car!" The driver demanded. When his confused passenger didn't comply fast enough, he got out and rushed around to her side.

"Hey! Where's my money!" Teresa complained as he pulled her from the car.

"Right here!" He said, while giving her a hard kick in her backside. He was still cursing and complaining as he pulled away.

Always a quick study, Teresa learned a lesson with her first trick. In crack-whore 101 you're taught to always get paid first. That's exactly what she did on her next trick which came as soon as she walked around the front.

"Shawty! Come here shawty!" A young dealer called from his room doorway. He couldn't believe his luck when the pretty woman emerged from the rear. He had just decided a blow job would ease the monotony of selling crack and here the woman appeared.

Teresa recognized him for the dealer he was and rushed over.

"Fifty bucks and I get paid first!" She demanded! In a, take it, or leave it tone. He took it.

"You want cash or work?" He asked lustfully, taking in her curves. Even in her Dollar Store clothes she still looked good.

"Half and half" Teresa replied as she could smell the fresh cut dope. "I would like to smoke before we get down to business."

"I ain't tryna breath that shit shawty, here!" The dealer frowned. He handed her three 'dime' size bags and a twenty dollar bill. He came out of his clothes so quickly Clark Kent would have been proud.

He was also impressed when she slipped out of her clothing. Most junkies around didn't have much weight on them unless they just got out of jail. A newly released addict could charge top dollar until she smoked herself back to a skeleton.

"Oh!" Teresa yelped when the dealer shoved his hand into her crotch. He inhaled his fingers savoring the clean smell.

"My name Flava," he said seductively as he made the decision to make love to the rare find. Of course making love to him meant fucking her raw. Teresa's mind was on the dope she clutched tightly in her hand.

Flava 'oohed' and 'ahhed' having a great time inside of Teresa. He was hitting it so well that she actually had an orgasm followed closely by his. The dealer rested for a minute inside of her until she gently nudged him off. Good pussy is like a sedative and will put you right to sleep.

"Thanks but I must go now," Teresa said politely. Still hungry she decided to eat something before smoking her pay.

"Fuck with me later" Flava offered and got dressed as quickly as he had disrobed. Without bothering to wash the mess of their combined fluids off of him.

"Uh...Ok" she replied doing the same.

Once outside the plan to eat first was short lived when she spotted a well-worn smoker going into a room.

"Excuse me, do you have a pipe? I'll share a hit with you." She asked sweetly.

"Sho nuff!" The big headed little junky said enthusiastically, as if her winning lottery ticket had been called.

In a way it had. There wasn't enough left on old Shirley to fuck so she had struck out on her quest to turn a trick.

"Sho? Umm...nuff." Teresa replied and followed her inside. If you've seen one ghetto motel you've seen them all, still Teresa fought the natural gag reflex from the strong odors.

Having cuffed two of her sacks with the adeptness of a magician, Teresa produced the remaining dime. She cut it not quite in half and greedily sucked it up. As much as she hated to she handed over the balance.

The long overdue hit changed all plans, even chasing the hunger pains away. Not satisfied with half a rock she produced another, then another, then spent the twenty. An hour after arriving at the hotel she was back to zero.

Less than zero actually, considering what was to come.

Chapter 28

"That's her right there!" Flava said just below a yell as he and a carload of friends pulled up.

It was a stroke of luck, both good and bad that the horny hoodlums pulled up just as Teresa decided she would turn a trick or two, just enough to get her through the night.

"She straight!" One of his partners agreed after grabbing a handful of Teresa's ass.

"I'm sorry I won't be able to accommodate all of you gentlemen, but you and I can repeat our earlier arrangement." Teresa explained.

The six young men starred curiously at each other and then to her for translation to 'hood' speech.

"Hold up shawty, I'll be back," Flava said rushing her to his room.

He understood the part of him fucking. And fuck he did. Flava got his money's worth as he fucked her every which way he could think of. He paid her in all crack, and Teresa rushed past to go smoke.

All of the others propositioned her for a ride on their dicks but she was moving too fast to hear. She wasn't moving fast enough not to be recognized though.

"Dats dat bitch rat dere dat robbed me!" Milo fumed upon seeing her.

"Who dat J?" Tip laughed not because it was funny but because he laughed at everything.

"Yeah, bitch got me 'fo like 5 ounces." Milo lied hoping to make his friends think he was moving more work than them; they didn't buy it. "I'm finna get dat bitch!"

"Only five ounces you had was the last time you took a shit!" Flava announced sending Tip back into another laughing spell.

"Chill shawty, too much money out here to be worried 'bout them five sacks she got you 'fo. Lil mama got some good pussy, but she only fuck with me."

132

"Shit I'm tryna touch something my damn self!" Tip laughed grabbing his crotch.

"Dere go mama," Flava said pointing to an ancient crack head everyone called 'Mama'.

She was only in her late fifties but life on the streets added twenty more years to her once was pretty face.

Mama was living proof that practice makes perfect. After almost twenty years of turning tricks she was said to have the best head north of the equator. The crew of young goons would have preferred a romp with still sexy Teresa but settled for Mama.

Once inside the room Mama lined them up and knocked them down. She had long lost the dentures she used as collateral for drugs for which she didn't pay, but there was nothing in her way. It was lips, tongue, throat, hand, next! While youngins got their rocks off.

They paid her a sack each once they were done. Once she was done she took her 8 sacks to smoke with her buddy Shirley.

"Hey gurl," Mama said cheerfully as Shirley stepped aside to let her in the room. Her breath was tart from the boys' semen but Mama had her 'I got some rocks' walk. It was an odd little hobble with one leg stiff which signified she had some dope.

"You ok Mama? Get her a glass of water." Shirley said worried about getting high more than her ailing friend.

"Teresa?" Mama cried after a few sips of the water eased her burning throat.

"Yeah?" Teresa questioned wondering how the woman knew her name.

'The news!' She thought near panic. *'No Shirley must have told her'*

She settled upon her host telling the vaguely familiar woman her name.

"Do I know you?" Teresa asked curtly.

"Err body knows Mama," Mama said softly in a familiar voice. She fought back a tear when she watched Teresa load a rock onto the shooter and inhale it.

The mood was subdued until the woman ran out of dope. They sat around for a few minutes pretending they were done for the night until Shirley spoke up.

"I guess I'll suck a few sacks out of one dese young boys," she announced.

"Reckon I'm finna do the same," Mama sighed.

"Teresa, since you're our guest you just hold down the fort." Shirley offered.

"Umm...well ok." Teresa agreed.

She was relieved not to have hit the trenches with the veteran street walkers even though she accepted her fate. She knew it was just a matter of time.

It took Teresa exactly ten minutes of being alone before she decided to act. A quick romp with Flava and a few rocks would tie her over until her new friends returned. Of course they didn't need to know about her earnings.

"Excuse me young man, is Mr. Flava around?" Teresa asked the lone remaining dealer.

"Err body went to the club," Milo snarled.

He was hot about being left behind and now seeing the woman who stole his dope. Flava's warning about leaving her alone flashed in his mind but disappeared just as quickly.

"You wouldn't happen to have any product you would like to barter for do you?" Teresa said seductively.

The young thug had no idea what she had just said as his vocabulary was limited to his favorite rapper. He was able to ascertain that it was English but beyond that nothing.

"Sex! Would you like some sex for drugs?" She spelled out.

"I'll take a lil cap for a sack or two" he replied. Now it was her turn to be bewildered. "Suck a nigga dick or something." That she understood.

"Make it three and you have a deal!"

"That's what up!" Milo agreed although he didn't plan paying her anything.

The way he figured, she owed him, a free blow job would settle the score. Teresa took him to Shirley's room hoping to get him off and smoke at least one rock before the women returned. Once inside she quickly ushered him to the back of her throat.

Milo intended to punish the woman and forcefully grabbed her head. He savagely slammed into her face gagging her with each stroke.

"Suck dat shit bitch!" He demanded, "Damn junky bitch!"

The word junky touched Teresa to her very core. Like it or not that's what she had become. Her job, home, husband, children all replaced for dope, and the vile little boy humping her face.

She vowed then to get clean, and go home. The police had a weak case against her and she knew it. Besides, who could play victim better than her. Not to mention she was the daughter of the renowned Reverend McCoy.

Besides she was a preacher's wife, and it ain't easy being a preacher's wife. Besides...

"Un uh take it bitch!" Milo demanded as he pushed into her tonsils and came.

Teresa nearly choked as the boy cut off her wind with his penis and semen. Finally the spasms sending a torrent of cum down her throat eased, and he began to deflate.

She still resolved to go home as this was no life for her, but she was gonna smoke her last rocks first.

"Well, thank you. I'll take my pay now please." Teresa asked as Milo tucked himself back into his pants.

"Bitch I ain't giving you shit!" He spat then spat in her face. "You owed me that for dem rocks you stole over on the block."

Teresa had no idea what he meant, but he was not leaving without paying her. She grabbed his shirt as he turned to leave, but a vicious back hand caused her to turn it loose.

"Bitch keep yo damn junky hands off me!" he demanded.

There was that word again, Teresa thought as the hard slap sent her across the small room. She landed on the table on top of the knife Shirley kept for protection. Instinctively, she grabbed it and sprang into action. She caught him right as he reached for the door knob.

"Bitch!" Milo screamed as the semi sharp knife entered his back. He spun away with it still embedded in his body.

As he struggled to pull the foreign object from his back Teresa clawed at his face. He managed to free it and in one quick thrust impaled his attacker in her throat. Milo ran from the room as Teresa slowly sank to the filthy carpet.

The large spurts of blood each time her heart beat told her that an artery was hit. She didn't have much time.

"Oh my god!" mama yelled as she came into the blood soaked room. She rushed to her side and tried to stop the profuse bleeding with her small hands.

"It's ok, mama's here" she comforted. It was at that moment Teresa realized, mama really was her mama. Here was her long lost mother desperately trying to save her life. Or, so she thought. She tried to speak but the horrific injury prevented it.

"Uh uh don't talk baby, its ok. Mama's here," mama cooed.

She gently covered her daughter's mouth and pinched closed her nostrils. This was better than the jail cell that awaited her. Far better than the near hell existence as a drug addict. Who would know better than she? Would her child be here if she wasn't?

"I know baby, I know. Just let it go baby," she comforted as her only child left the earth for what comes next.

"I told you, it ain't easy being a preacher's wife."

Epilogue

"Yeah," said Edwin now that that bitch is dead I can breathe easy." Reverend Cash nodded as he drove.

"She ain't have nothing on you, I was the one worried." Edwin added

"True but if you go down I go down. That's what you said ain't it!" Cash spat.

"Yeah, but I..."

"Naw, it's cool. We're good. After tonight err thing will be cool. No more worries after tonight." He assured him.

Edwin felt a chill from the ominous tones in which the Pastor spoke. He instantly regretted making the threat to the dangerous man.

"Say where we headed?" Edwin asked as Cash pulled off on MLK into the heart of the hood.

"Quick stop to tie up one last loose end," Cash replied. He dug into his inside pocket causing Edwin to hold his breath. Instead of a gun like his passenger feared, he came out with a sizeable bankroll.

"Here we go," Cash said as he tossed the money to him.

"What's this for?" Edwin asked frowning at the cash.

"Payment," Cash replied as he lowered the window and pulled to the curb.

"Payments for w...." was all he got out before a man appeared from the shadows. He rushed the car and shot Edwin in his temple before he could finish the question.

"Your murder," Cash laughed as the hired gun scooped the money from his dead hand.

Yeah Reverend Cash is a damn trip. A killer, a thug, a thief, and a womanizer among other things. But....that's another story.

REVEREND CASH.....NEXT!

Little Miss Molly

Sa'id Salaam

"O you who believe, intoxicants, and

gambling, and the altars of idols, and the
games of chance are abominations of the
devil; you shall avoid them, that you may
succeed."

The Qur'an 5:90

molly

**Abr. of 'molecular'.
Pure form of MDMA
(ecstasy), usually a free
powder or in capsules.
Oftentimes MDA is sold as
molly. Should be white in
color (when it's pure) but is
more often beige or yellow-
brown, and sometimes
brown or rarely gray**

.

Prologue

"Oh my god!" Mama yelled as she came into the blood soaked room. She rushed to her daughter's side and tried to stop the bleeding with her small hands.

Teresa looked up and realized that the little crack head caring for her was indeed her long lost mama. The horrific injury to her throat prevented her from speaking so she batted her eyes.

"I know baby I know," mama cooed. Knowing the two fates that awaited her daughter if she survived mama made a decision. She gently covered her mouth and pinched her nostrils close. Death would be better than life in jail or even worse, a crack head.

"Just let it go, let go," mama said gently. "I know it aint easy being a preacher's wife."

Teresa felt her wicked soul being pulled out of the body and relaxed. Just before leaving she blinked one final message, "It aint easy being a preacher's daughter either."

Chapter 1

"What in the world make you throw all of this away?" Mrs. Morris wondered aloud as she opened the door to the Sanders home. The social worker was assigned the case and was tasked with delivering the now orphaned Sanders children to their grandparents.

"Why can't we just stay here? I'm 16, I can take care of my brother and I," Hazel demanded like the spoiled little diva that she was.

She had grown into a gorgeous young woman with her father's smooth chocolate hue and athletic traits. The pretty face and curvy little body she got from her mother. Her face was framed by a crop of thick, well maintained hair. Even though she had the hips, ass and breast of a woman she still had a childlike innocence to her. That was courtesy of a proper environment despite the evil that lay underneath. Unfortunately that s not all she inherited from the woman. That's the way evil is though, it can't remain hidden forever. Sooner or later it's going to manifest itself and destroy everything around it.

"I have no doubt that you are capable of taking care of yourself and your brother, however the law requires you to have a guardian until you're 18," Mrs. Morris replied.

She looked over to the stoic little boy and frowned internally. She gleamed from investigation that he was not Reverend Sander's biological child and with the mother deceased, chances are he would never find his real father. The handsome 12 year old had a sadness to him that broke the woman's heart. In fact, the story of 'THE PREACHERS WIFE' was the saddest she'd ever heard. Straight chronicles of a junky.

"So when I turn 18 we can come back?" Hazel asked hopefully. As much as she adored her grandfather and sister Clarice she had no desire to live with them. A trip to the ghetto to visit them was like a trip to the zoo. The hood was full of animals foreign to what she called life.

"I don't see why not?" Mrs. Morris replied she of course had no way of knowing that the bank swooped in to take what was theirs. Or that the revised will left everything to his other family. "Now hurry and gather what you want to take with you."

"Ok," Calvin sang in a soft voice. He breezed off with the aire of feminity of a budding homosexual. The molestation he suffered at the hands of the deceased church accountant left him confused. He lived under a fog of shame, anger, curiosity and worst of all desire.

Hazel was still a virgin as her busy schedule had zero time for boys. The preacher and his wife were fucked up people but ironically very good parents. They kept their children busy in a variety of activities.

"Ok, can I take a last look around?" Hazel pleaded.

"Sure," The social worker relented. "Take your time."

Hazel rushed up to her room and tried to pack the entire room. She pulled her ERV-G and Doobie Daddy posters from the wall and rolled them up. She stuffed what she could into her luggage then garbage bags once they were full.

Calvin packed his favorite clothes and games and took them to the car. When he finished he began to help his sister. He moaned like a girl as he struggled with the heavy bags. Once they were loaded up it was time to leave.

"Wait! I forgot my ....um..." Hazel announced and ran back into the house. She took the stairs by twos. She had tried to ignore the crime scene that was once her parent's room but couldn't. Hazel turned the knob and timorously entered.

"Dang daddy," she moaned at the large section of missing carpet that marked his murder.

There was one more missing section for that of his killer. She opened his closet and ran her hands through the line of suits that kept her handsome father dapper. The thought of him up on that pulpit spitting the gospel brought a smile to her face.

That smile quickly dissipated when she reached her mother's clothes. The beautiful woman wore the sharpest clothes but she destroyed herself. A picture on her mother's night stand caught her eye and called her over. It was the Sanders family in happier times. Mom had a healthy glow of sobriety as she held a young Calvin while dad proudly hugged his darling daughter.

The drawer to the night stand was open and invited Hazel to look inside. Inside was sex toys of different sizes shapes and colors. Along with flavored gels and lubricants.

"Oh my!" Hazel exclaimed when she picked up a ten inch latex penis. "How could this possibly fit into someone?"

Hazel studied the large dildo with a curious frown. A twist of the knob at the end put the huge dick in motion. It made a slow spiral motion and vibrated at the base. It was still slightly sticky from the orgasms that movement got out of her mother. She turned it off and picked up a cute pink one. It was considerably smaller and thinner. She was about to turn the knob to see what tricks this one could do but was interrupted.

"Hazel darling, we really must be getting on our way" Mrs. Morris urged from the door way.

"Ok!" Hazel replied shoving the sex toy into her pocket so not to be seen. She had no choice now except to keep it so she lowered her head and walked past. Curiosity got the best of the social worker so she walked over to investigate.

"Oh my!" she exclaimed at the sight of the 10 inch job. She shot a glance around then put in her purse.

Chapter 2

Life in the McCoy home had changed drastically since Teresa grew up there. The biggest change was that the once prominent pastor was near broke. Competition from the mega churches had reduced his congregation to a Skelton.

The younger, hipper worshippers had fled to the trendy churches with celebrity pastors and reality shows. They left their roots along with parents and grandparents. The elderly congregation put what they could afford from retirement and S.S.I checks into the basket but it wasn't much. Since the congregation was elderly it was reduced once a month by a death. At least pastor McCoy earned a few extra coins by doing a funeral. In a neighborhood of baby mamas and baby daddies there were few weddings.

~~~~

"Hey grandma, hey grandpa!" Calvin cheered as he burst into the house. He skipped over to hug sister Clarice as the pastor frowned.

The man had lived in Atlanta long enough to know a sissy when he saw one. Especially with one living next door. He had no way of knowing that Darrin rarely interacted with the boy leaving him to emulate his mother and sister.

Hazel wanted to cry when she walked into her grandparent's home. It suddenly looked rundown now that it was home. Her old home smelled of potpourri and pot roast while this one smelled like collard greens and old folks. Life had just taken a turn for the worse but the worst was yet to come, Chronicles of a junky worse.

"You guys have my number so call me anytime," Mrs. Morris offered sincerely. She hugged the kids and shook Pastor and sisters hands before departing.

Hazel did cry when she entered her new bedroom which was her mother's old bedroom. She didn't even bother to unpack before diving into the twin bed to cry her eyes out.

Pastor McCoy could no longer afford private school so the children would be forced to enter the fucked up city of Atlanta schools. They were both in for the culture shock of their lives.

Calvin would be attending Martin Luther King middle school. The school was so bad its name sake might dig himself out of his own grave and say 'yall take my name off that shit!' It was in walking distance so young Calvin walked. Poor thing didn't make it all the way inside before getting his ass kicked.

"Hey guys, I'm Calvin!" He greeted a small crowd of boys smoking weed before school. "Is that pot!"

"Who dis nigga?" Their leader wanted to know. He took one look at his brand new uniform and Jordans and decided, "He must be a sissy talking like that!"

"Sound like a sissy. Let's kick his ass," A third recommended. The suggestion set off his first ass kicking of the school year. It would be the last.

Since the school was walking distance Calvin walked home minus his tenis shoes to change clothes. The next door neighbor was pulling out of the driveway when he saw the beat up boy.

"Un uh! Who did this to you?" He demanded, flailing his hand and popping his fingers.

"Some boys at school they took my shoes?" Calvin replied astonished.

"Well go inside and get changed. Uncle Maurice finna take your back and read them!" He insisted.

Maurice did just that and got his shoes back. He gave him his phone number and invited him to come down to his hair salon. That's how it started.

~~~~

Hazel didn't fare much better on her first day at Washington High school. It was named after Denzel, not George. Since there were more kids out of school then in, several schools were closed and combined. They closed schools and built prisons.

The violent, drug infested school was too far to walk so she walked to the bus stop. Students were given free passes to ride the city buses for free. Like her brother she was in some shit before she even reached school.

"Who dis bitch?" A girl frowned as Hazel approached.

"Oh she think she cute!" Another observed. And she was cute even in the school uniform.

The city of Atlanta wisely opted to force kids to wear uniforms so students would be dressed uniformly. You know the cool ghetto kids had to pimp their clothes. The boys wore the pants a couple sizes up and hanging off their asses. The girls hemmed skirts to mid thigh or low crotch and half button shirts to show cleavage.

Hazel's uniform was worn properly at the knee and buttoned to her neck. It was the matching Coach bag and shoes that got her hated on. Then the ratchet girls couldn't see any weave hump and really got mad. This chick has the nerve to have real hair! How dare her! Bitch!

Hazel tried to ignore the girls and cracked a half smile at a pretty brown girl covered except for her cute face. The girl cracked a duplicate half smile and turned back to the remembrance of her lord. She used the finger of her right hand and moved her lips.

The girls loudly ridiculed her the entire ride to school. Having English first period brought a smile to Hazels face. This was her favorite subject, until now that is.

"Hey y'all, its mi mall and I'se yo teacher fo first period English" a young woman who looked like something out of a low budget rap video. She had red weave piled high on her head and dressed like a hoochie mama.

"You cannot be serious!" Hazel said hotly. "You aren't even speaking English!"

"Yes I'm is!" The teacher shot moving her neck back and forth like only a ghetto girl can.

"Dat bitch dink she betta dan us!" A student demanded from the back.

Hazel may have fared better had she not opened her mouth. Now she had everyone full attention. All eyes were now upon the pretty, brown girl, with thick brown hair. The boys all wanted to fuck her and the girls all wanted to fuck her up.

"Who is you?" The teacher frowned looking at her roster to match a name with the trouble maker. Hazel stood, smiled and drew inspiration from drama class.

"Well, I'm Hazel Sanders. 16, from Sugar Hill, Sugar hill in Gwinnett that is not the ghetto one." She said frowning up at the thought.

"Who dis bitch 'posed to be?" A girl named Shanadoa said taking to her cheap sandaled feet.

"Bitch?" Hazel asked indignantly and paid for it instantly.

"Who you calling a bitch? Bitch!" she said crossing the room like weaved lighting.

The wild little ghetto girl was on her ass so fast she didn't know what hit her. Jealous girls always go for the hair and face first. Shanadoa tried to pull a plug out of her hair but the regular salon treatments had it healthy as a horse. The false nail attack on her face was foiled as well. Hazel used her athletic legs to shove the girl across the room. Security rushed in like a prison tactical team and broke it up.

In a school that actually had a murder rate a fight is no big deal. The combatants were taken counselor who told them to shake hands and guided them back to class. The word spread like wild flowers and by the end of the day everyone was waiting on a show down.

"There she goes Twan," City boy said to his boss. Antwan was a student himself but his hustling business required side kicks and flunkies. City boy was both.

"Got damn she fine!" He exclaimed when he pointed out Hazel. The hustla hustled petty drugs and pretty girls. His best seller was pussy but since he didn't have one of his own he sold O.P.P. That's other people's pussy for those too young to remember the song. He wasn't the only pussy peddler in school.

"Dere go that bitch rat dere!" A little rachet girl announced to alert Shanadoa and company. The group of girls who would only rise to baby mama status in life moved in to whoop Hazel's ass.

"Bitch think she pretty, bitch think she cute. That bitch tried me." They murmured as they approached. They drew closer and closer then stopped dead in their tracks. A look of sheer horror spread on all faces and they scattered in different directions.

"What the ...?" Hazel demanded feeling a hand reach under her skirt and palm an ass cheek.

"Not what, who," The hands owner replied when she spun around. "The answer to that question is sucka-fish."

Hazel winced from the name and its owner. It took several blinks to ascertain that this cute guy was actually a girl. A stud to be precise. She stood five foot, nine inches and sported a low cut faded Mohawk. She tried to down play being a pretty girl by wearing baggy clothes on her shapely body and a scowl on her oval face. Neither really worked but a well known violent streak did the trick.

The name sucka-fish actually started out as a diss when she got caught eating some pussy in middle school. The kids called her suck her fish but she embraced it and made it her own. At first you got beat up for calling her by that name, now you could get beat up for not calling her it.

"Well your hand...is on my ass!" Hazel said pushing it away.

"My hand was on my ass. I just saved it for you cuz trust and believe them hoes were going to beat it!" She said in her odd voice. Sucka-fish tried to lower her voice a few octaves but the feminine timbre could still be heard underneath. "Or would you rather I call that lil pack of hood rats back over."

"No!" She snapped. The girls paced with ice grills, mad that they couldn't get at her. Hazel wasn't sure what she did to make them hate her but hate her they did. She didn't know they were haters so they were just doing their job. The mind of a hater is still a medical mystery.

"Aight, you on my team now and nobody fucks with my team!"

"Team?" Hazel asked eagerly. She was on several teams back home. "What do I have to do?"

"Nothing yet" Sucka-fish said. She saw how green she was and knew she had to move slow. A glance over at Antwan staring told her she needed to move fast. "Here take my card and give me a call."

Hazel watched as the stud rejoined two identical twins dressed identically. They all jumped into a convertible BMW and pulled away. Hazel boarded the bus and stayed in front away from the hood rats in the back. With no other choice she sat next to the Muslim girl from her block.

"Why can't you people eat pork?" Hazel demanded with a mask of disdain on her face.

"Fatimah and what's your name" the girl replied with a hint of sarcasm.

"Hazel and what's wrong with pork?" She came back.

"Simply because God said don't eat it" Fatimah answered.

"That's it!" Hazel asked assuming there was some mystical, magical answer.

"That's it."

Chapter 3

Hazel came home to find her grandfather underneath his car trying to fix whatever was wrong with it. Gone were the days of new Caddie from the congregation. As were the days of extra cash to put the car in the shop. Not knowing any of that she marched right up and made her demands.

"Grandfather, I need..." she began and didn't stop. Her poor in more ways than one grandfather listened to a long list of stuff he couldn't afford. He never heard of most of the things but was pretty sure he couldn't afford them.

Reverend McCoy displayed a soft smile to hide the pain and embarrassment. When he felt he could not longer bat back the tears, he turned and walked into the house. Hazel looked puzzled and turned to Sister Clarice on the porch.

"Forgive your grandpa, he's a proud man. Truth is the church done fell on hard times. We're barely getting by."

"That's ok, we can get jobs and help out!" Calvin cheered enthusiastically.

"Eww!" Hazel frowned, turning her nose up at the notion of getting a job. She was a spoiled diva use to getting whatever she wanted. That was going to cost her a hell of a lot more than a job would.

~~~~

The effects of being under Sucka-fish's protection was immediately evident. When Hazel went to the bus stop the haters hated but no one said shit. They had a problem with her Gucci loafers and purse but kept it to themselves.

The bus arrived just in time to see Sucker-fish and the twins pull up in yet another expensive vehicle. The twins wore tight white jeans matching the stud's sweat suit. Sucka-fish saw Hazel getting off the bus and blew her a kiss.

The sidity girl turned her nose up at Sister Clarice's grits hoping to get better at school breakfast. She should have eaten those grits because the ones at school were lumpy and watered down. She ate half a biscuit and went to class.

By lunch Hazel's stomach loudly complained about being hungry. Pride wasn't filling so she swallowed it and took her place in the free lunch line. Line isn't the best word for the mob of unruly ghetto kids. They pushed, shoved and skipped to get to the front.

Hazel looked down at the thing on her tray they called pizza. The square bread had a dab of red stuff and square of cheese. With hunger the only other option she chomped into it. As she chewed the card board crust she saw Sucka-fish.

The stud and twins skipped the line to the schools grill. Kids with money or parents with money could order fresh off the grill burgers and the like. She pulled out a large roll of cash and paid for more food than they could possibly eat.

"Join us," Sucka-fish suggested as they walked passed her seated alone.

"No thank you, I have pizza!" Hazel declined politely and took a smiling bite.

After a week of disgusting food Hazel finally took the stud up on her offer. She sat there under the intense stares of the twins as she ate her chicken fingers.

"I'm Hazel and you guys are...? She asked.

"I'm Summer and she's Eve" The first twin replied. It was all she could do not to cough her food back up at the sound of the names. Who would name their children after a douche? Even worse they had another sister in middle school named massengale.

"So when you gone come hang out with us?" Sucka-fish asked. She got the hook in her mouth when she accepted the food, now it was time to snatch her ass out of the water.

"Um..." Hazel pondered on declining but a quick once over of the twins changed her mind. Both girls rocked Stella McCartney purses that she knew ran a grand and better.

"Whenever!" She cheered.

"Cool, my people are having a little house party Saturday. I'll come get you" The stud said and stood.

"Ok, I'll call and let you know where I live."

"I already know where you stay," she smiled and walked off. She had been followed the bus then followed the girl to her house. She wasn't the only one either.

"Look like ole Sucka-fish gonna suck that fish!" City boy told Antwan.

"Everything in time shawty. I'ma let her turn the hoe and I'ma scoop her up," Antwan nodded.

~~~~

When Saturday rolled around Hazel dressed conservatively in a Dolce and Gabana skirt and top with matching sandals. She nearly panicked when she heard the door bell followed by Sister Clarice yelling her name.

"Shit!" she cursed trying to figure out how she could explain Sucka-fish. To her relief it was Eve, or Summer, one of them standing in the living room.

Sucka-fish learned from bad experiences to send one of her girls in for new girls. No parent wants some stud licking their baby's box. She made a quick introduction and led the twin outside.

"You look...um?" Sucka-fish said getting stuck looking for an adjective.

"Overdressed?" Hazel offered looking at what they were wearing. The twins had on matching tennis skirts and tight polo shirts. Sucka-fish rocked a pair of baggy jeans and Hawks jersey over a large white t-shirt. They were all in costume.

Once they got in the car and underway Summer pulled a small capsule from her purse. She opened it and dumped half of the power content on her hand between thumb and index finger. Eve extended her
hand and got the same.

"Have some?" Summer asked as they licked the powder from each
others hand.

"Is that cocaine!" Hazel exclaimed ready to leap from the moving
car.

"Hell naw! Don't nobody fuck with no coke!" Sucka-fish spat
forcefully. Like Hazel and so many others cocaine fucked up her parents and in turn fucked up her life.

"Just some Molly," Eve said innocuously.

"Oh, ok," Hazel relaxed. She of course heard of it going to school
with wealthy white kids. It was actually the drug of choice in her old
school.

"Here, take a few sips of this, you gotta lighten up." Sucka-fish said
passing her the wine cooler from between her legs.

"Thanks," she smiled accepting it. She had a glass of wine on quite a
few occasions with her parents. Only those weren't laced with MDMA.

Sucka-fish smiled internally at the first step in turning the pretty
girl out. Summer and Eve were bad bitches in the ghetto, hood rats'
sense. They were easy to flip since they had been dogged out by so many
dudes. Their low morals and base desires made them easy prey. Guys
fucked them for blunts and trinkets but Sucka-fish put clothes on their
backs and cash in their purses. That and feeding their substance abuse
problems.

"Here we go" Sucka-fish announced as they pulled into an upscale
sub-division. Hazel felt a stab of home-sickness looking at the half million dollar homes like the one she recently called home.

She pulled as close as possible to the last home in a cul-de-sac
and parked. The million dollars worth of luxury cars in the driveway

and lining the street spelled rich people. Her type of people, or so she thought.

A warm glow spread smile came on Haze's face as she began to feel the effects of the molly laced cooler. The trio played follow the leader to the house and let Sucka-fish ring the bell.

"Evening ladies and gen...? An elderly butler greeted getting stuck on the stud appearance. "Um, this way."

Hazel noticed several sophisticated ladies chatting as they made their way through the home. What she didn't notice was any men. They made it to the large den and there weren't any men in there either. Just more rich, late thirty and forty-something women. The room erupted in dainty applause when the women saw Sucka-fish.

"Y'all bitches ain't ready for Sucka-fish!" The stud demanded taking control of the room. The challenge sent a ripple of cheers through the women.

The lady of the house hit a button on a huge remote control that filled the room with music. Sucka-fish jumped on top of a large wooden coffee table and went in. She went through of medley of hip-hop dances to the hip-hop music blaring through the speakers. The women old enough to be her mother cheered and threw money at her.

This wasn't like a male strip club with cheap dudes tossing ones and an occasional five. No, these horny old broads were throwing nothing but twenties. Summer and Eve got to work collecting the money as Hazel sat next to a pretty lady smiling and clapping.

Sucka-fish jumped down from the table and began to work the room. She danced up on different women who cheered, felt on her and stuffed money in her pockets. As she worked the crowd she shed clothing. Finally she was reduced to a wife beater and boxer briefs with a long lump in it.

"Ok, you know what we want to see!" The host announced changing the music to slow grooves. She dimmed the lights to set the mood.

Summer and Eve got into the show. Eve tugged the stud's boxers down causing a large strap on to pop out. More money rained when the twins took turns sucking it. The women, most of whom were married and left real dicks at home cheered wildly at the spectacle.

It really turned up when the twins stripped to nothing and the stud lay flat on her back. Eve stepped over her face and lowered her box onto her mouth. She hissed loudly when Sucka-fish clamped her lips on her vagina. Summer lowered herself on to the huge strap on. The girl was pretty on the outside but obviously hollow in the inside because she fit the whole thing inside of her.

The crowd watched in awe at the girl-girl action on the floor. More than a few hands slipped under skirts and pant suits to masturbate along with them. The women seated next to Hazel crossed her legs and squeezed and released until she came with a whimper.

Eve came with a howl that shook the room. Her sister was right behind her as she rode the dildo to an orgasm. Hazel felt crazy from all the new sights. She was confused but never happier in her life.

The show was more like a paid commercial. After it was over Sucka-fish took numbers and had discreet conversations with almost half of the twenty women. The highest bidder arranged for private show later that night. After dropping her crew off Sucka-fish was going to suck new life into her 50 year old box.

Chapter 4

"Have fun?" Sucka-fish asked, breaking the silence as they drove back into the city.

"I um... yes," Hazel stammered trying to get a grip on exactly what she was feeling. Happy didn't quite tell it, it felt as if she had an electric current running through her. A current that turned her on for the first time in her preoccupied life.

"Good, I'm glad." The stud nodded turning her attention back to the road while Summer and Eve bantered about the latest fashions.

"Well thanks guys, we um gotta...yeah." Hazel mumbled when Sucka-fish turned on to her street. She did have fun but had no intention of going anywhere with them ever again. If her only choices were the gay girls of the hood rats she would just have to be home schooled.

"Thanks," Sucka-fish said handing her two hundred of the two thousand dollars she made. Summer and Eve would each get twice that with the lions share going to the star of the show. Plus thousand dollars the woman was paying her to suck her fish.

"What's this for?" Hazel asked as she took the money. She frowned seeing her brother exit the neighbor's house and run into their grandparents.

"Your share, you're part of the team. We eat, you eat" the stud stated with the twins nodding in agreement.

"Ok, thanks," Hazel said dryly and got out. She rushed to the house quickly to distance herself. No way was she a part of any vagina eating, plastic dick riding team. Not to mention the buzzing between her legs needed to be investigated.

A shower did nothing to calm her throbbing box. It got worse when she touched it with the wash cloth and made her knees buckle. Even toweling off after the shower didn't help. It did nothing to make it dry. She decided to jump in bed and hide from the sensation but it found her under the covers.

"Maybe I can rub it away," Hazel thought aloud. She slipped a hand between her legs and rubbed it until it burst.

"What the heck was that!" Hazel wondered once she stopped shaking. She lifted her hand to examine the gush of fluid on it.

Hazel knew enough to know she had just bust a nut and it felt great! Just to make sure it wasn't a fluke she did it again and got the same results. She suddenly remembered the dildo she took from her late mothers night stand.

"Shit!" The girl cursed when a twist of the knob at the base got no results. She banged on it a few times before checking the batteries. A search for batteries came up empty so she took some out of the remote. "There we go!"

Hazel played around with the vibrating device fighting the urge to insert it. In the end she kept her virginity in place by not entering herself.

~~~~

The next afternoon when Hazel awoke alone in the house, feeling crazy. All the events of her short life echoed through her mind ending in the death of both parents and the loss of her own lifestyle. The severe depression propelled her into her grandparent's medicine cabinets.

Had there been the drugs to do it this short story would be a lot shorter because she had every intention of killing herself. A search of the dresser draw produced a hand gun. The disconsolate girl put it to her temple and pulled the trigger. Then again, and once again.

"I can't even kill myself!" She moaned and broke down into sob. Hazel sat there crying for hours. It wasn't until she heard the family return that she returned the gun to the drawer and returned to her room.

"What the hell is wrong with me?" Hazel questioned then googled the term. The search came up with a bunch of silly blogs but no answer until the end of the page. "Suicide Tuesday?"

She grew heated reading the effects and side effects of the drug ec-stasy. This was why she was so happy last night and sad today as her body went through withdrawals. She almost called Sucka-fish to give her a piece of her mind but when she remembered the stud she remem-bered the money. She quickly decided to wait til school; she had some shopping to do.

"I'm going to the mall," Hazel announced breezing through the liv-ing room.

"Take me! Please, please," Calvin pleaded bouncing up and down.

"No!"

"Yes!" Grandpa insisted." He can look after you."

"Come on boy." Hazel moaned and led her little brother up the street to the bus stop. "And I don't have any money for you!"

"I have my own money. Maurice gave me some."

~~~~

"So why must you wear all those clothes? You must be hot!" Hazel de-manded when she sat next to Fatimah on the bus.

"Actually blocking the sun from my skin keeps me cooler but its 90 degrees! Everyone is hot!" She explained reasonably. "Not to mention God commands us to."

"Whatever," Hazel huffed and inserted her ear buds. She listened to soft rock for the ride to school.

It wasn't until lunch time that Hazel saw Sucka-fish and the twins. By then she decided to let it go and ignore them. She acted like she didn't even see them when she got into the line for gilled food.

"Un uh! Did you see that? Lil Miss Thang did not just turn her nose up at us!" Summer protested.

"With her knock off Dooney & Bourke!" Eve nodded.

"Nah, that aint no knock off, and she cool," Sucka-fish replied. A broke girl with expensive taste is the easiest to pull. "Trust me, she'll be back."

"Thank you," Hazel told the confused cashier who had never once heard a student utter those words.

She took the change from the last twenty and shook her head. At six bucks for lunch it would not last the week. Hazel cast a glance to the loud, dirty kids in the free lunch line and sighed. That was her fate Thursday if nothing changed. With desperation setting in she decided to try her grandfather once more when she got home.

"Grandpa, could I use one of your credit cards? I need to pick up a few things" she said sweetly. It use to work like a charm with her dad.

"Credit card?" Pastor McCoy laughed. "Child I haven't had a credit in twenty years. Credit is the devil"

"It is," Calvin co-signed earning a nasty look.

Hazel stormed off hotly as she wasn't use to being told no. She had a major attitude brewing until inspiration struck. "Twenty years is long enough. Time for you to get a few cards."

~~~~

Hazel's plan required a little co-operation from her grandparents. She needed them to go to sleep so she could collect the information she needed to order a few cards. Easier said than done.

"It's your pussy!" Sister Clarice shouted in response to a question the good pastor asked during a good pounding. The sound of the bed squeaking and skin slapping echoed through the house but Hazel still pressed her ear to the door.

"I...said...who's...pussy...is...this!" He demanded punctuating each word with a thrust of his old hips.

"It's your pussy pastor! Get it, do what you want with it! Don't stop, get it, get it!" She shouted and threw it back.

An hour later the fucking stopped and the snoring began. Hazel crept in the room to get his wallet and got a little more than she bargained for. There was her grandfather laid on his back with his mouth wide open and big old dick laying on his belly. Sister Clarice was curled up in a fetal position sucking her thumb. The room had a musty smell of sex in the air.

Hazel found his wallet on the dresser and quickly copied all his vitals. She rushed back into her own room and went on-line. After filling out a joint application for instant credit she crossed her fingers and pressed 'enter.'

"Yes!" Hazel cheered when the application went through. She jumped up and spun around pumping her fist. When she finished celebration she sat back down and got back to work. By morning she had 10 credit cards en-route. Calvin loaned her twenty bucks to keep her out of the free lunch line and a week later they hit the mall.

Lenox mall was the place to be so it wasn't a surprise to run into people you knew. Hazel and Calvin had just parted near the food court when she was spotted by more than one interested party. Both made a bee-line but Sucka-fish made it there first. She stared at her fat ass switching from side to side as she rushed to catch up with her.

"Sup lil Miss Thang?" The stud asked running her eyes over the firm, young body.

"What is up is that you slipped me a molly when I specifically declined!" Hazel said with as much venom as she could muster.

"Slipped? Nah shawty, I thought you knew what I was sipping on. 'Sides I know you was rolling good!"

"Rolling good? I stayed up all night pla...um, I felt like crap in the morning. I've never been so depressed in my life!"

"That's cuz you let it stop. You gotta keep on rolling!" Sucka-fish encouraged and dug into the pocket of her over sized jeans. "Here"

Hazel debated with herself for what seemed like an eternity but in reality it was only a split second. The stuff did make her happier than ever in life. It did make her cum so hard tears came out of her eyes. She had been masturbating so much she ran the batteries out on the device and still couldn't duplicate what happened that first night. That's why she plucked the pills from her palm.

"You on the team shawty, you aint never gotta pay for that!" The stud offered.

"I have my own money, I can buy my own" Hazel replied holding up her bags as proof. She had just spent a couple of thousand dollars with the stolen credit cards.

"What's up shawty?" Antwan asked stepping between Hazel and Sucka-fish. "Look shawty I'll eat that pussy better than she can and lay this pipe. Plus, my money long."

"Get outta here Antwan!" The stud moaned in a rare display of feminity. Her eyes welled up ready to drop a tear.

"I'll let you guys talk," Hazel said and departed quickly. Both pimps pondered on her perfect ass until it was out of sight.

"Let that be the last time you try me," Sucka-fish growled with the unmistakable aire of violence.

"Whatever nigga. I'ma bag her, them ratchet ass twins, and you. I know you remember this dick!" Twan laughed.

"I don't remember shit about that lil ass dick," Sucka-fish lied. Of course she remembered losing her virginity to him years ago. Remembered loving him and getting dumped by him.

"Yeah, I know," Antwan laughed at the visible vulnerability and walked off.

"What that nigga talking 'bout?" Summer asked as she and Eve came over.

"Nothing! That nigga aint talkin 'bout shit!"

Chapter 5

Hazel had stepped into the bathroom and repeated what she had seen the twins do. She opened one of the capsules and dumped half of the powder on her hand and licked it off. She met her brother and boarded the bus to go home. Halfway there she was ecstatic and horney. She practically ran home from the bus stop. Calvin struggled to keep up with her with his bags full of beauty supplies.

Once they got home Hazel rushed to her room and scrambled to get the new batteries inside the vibrator. She only got one leg out of her jeans before pressing the humming device to her throbbing vagina. Her legs kicked violently and she let out a shriek when she came a minute later. She rested for a second then went for seconds. Would have went again if her brother wasn't calling her name and knocking on her door.

"Boy what!" She shouted at her brother then instantly regretted it. He was going through the same hardship as she was.

"I mean, what's up lil brother?"

"Can I do your hair?" He asked flamboyantly with a hand on his little hip. "I got my supplies!"

"Ok, come on," she said and followed him downstairs. The boy had set up his little beauty parlor in the dining room and was open for business.

"And so I read him his rights girl!" Calvin bantered on as he did his sisters hair. Their grandfather was in the kitchen with Clarice frowning deeply at the display.

"I think that boy is a sissy," the pastor said loud enough to be heard.

"To the hand," Calvin huffed throwing up his palm at the statement.

Hazel drank a gallon of juice to quench her thirst as her brother did her hair. He wanted to cut and color but had to settle for curls. An hour after he began he snatched the cape away and handed his sister a mirror.

"Oh boy, let's see what you...oh my!" Hazel exclaimed at the bouncy curls. "Calvin this is great!"

"Told you! Maurice taught me" he sang happily.

~~~~

Hazel rolled and shopped real good for about a week. Then the sit hit the fan and life got shitty. The amateur thief didn't cover her tracks well and her whole operation was quickly uncovered.

She sensed a problem when she got off the bus and saw an official looking car in the drive way. She wondered what it was about until she got inside. It was about her. The love seat was piled high with her new clothes and shoes. Another pile of clothes worn once sat on the floor.

"Why are my clothes here!" Hazel demanded. She looked at her grandparents, then the stranger.

"All of these items were fraudulently purchased" the white man announced sounding official.

"They wanted to lock you up girl!" Clarice said fearfully.

"Ain't nobody locking my baby up!" Pastor McCoy shouted. "We will pay for all this stuff.

"Well, the items with tags can simply be returned but..." The explanation was quickly interrupted by Hazel. The desperate girl rushed over and began snatching the tags off the clothes.

A wresting matched ensured with grandpa and Calvin eventually pulling her away. She shouted obscenities at all present and ran up stairs. Knowing a molly would make her feel better she rushed to get one in her system.

"Shit!" Hazel snapped when she realized this was her last capsule. She had been maintaining her high by constantly taking them. Being so anxious cost her and she dropped the capsule as soon as she cracked it open.

"Shit, shit!" She repeated watching the powder sink into the deep shag carpet. In her defining moment as a junky she dropped down to sniff and lick the ancient rug. She got nowhere and knew what she had to do.

~~~~

"What's up Lil Miss Molly?" Sucka-fish smiled when she took Hazel's call. The call was actually a day sooner than the projection she made based on the amount of drugs she gave her.

"I need...I want more. More molly" She admitted.

"No problem shawty! You know I got you, but..." the stud paused waiting to feel the nibble on her line. "I need a favor."

"But what? Sure anything. Team uh Sucka-fish," Hazel said since that's what she wanted to hear.

"I need you to come with me tonight. I got you on the pills, but I need you," Sucka-fish said yanking the hook deeply into her mouth.

"Sure, sure," she agreed. Anything to keep rolling.

"You wasting time on that hoe," Eve said when the line was closed.

"Shawty I'ma turn her tonight! Betcha that!"

~~~~

"Where's Summer's Eve?" Hazel asked when she sat into yet another fancy car driven by the young stud.

"They both got their period so they stayed in," she lied and pulled off. "Oh here."

Hazel snatched the drug offering and shamelessly dug in. The offset the mounting depression from withdrawals from the drug she ingested the whole thing. She cracked open the cap and dumped the contents into her mouth.

They rode over to mid-town and pulled up to a gated condo complex. Sucka-fish entered a code into the keypad causing the large iron gate to majestically open.

"Who lives here?" Hazel asked as they drove by Benzes, Acura's and Volvo's.

"Friend of mines. She asked me to drop by. Wish the twin's where here cuz she spends" Sucka-fish replied. She cast a side eye glance for reaction and saw the wheels were spinning.

They parked between the more luxury vehicles and got out. A smile turned Hazel's pretty lips ups as she felt the effects of the drug. Sucka-fish knocked on the door with the brass knocker and a older stud opened the door.

"Hey Sucka...oh my! What have we here? This is a marvelous creature!" She exclaimed.

The fifty something lesbian wore her grey hair in a throwback fresh prince high top fade. Many moons of practice gave her an authentic male swagger and husky voice. She ushered her guest into the den and offered wine.

"Thank you very much," Hazel said politely when she received her wine. Their host smiled at her proper diction and manners. She was use to the little ghetto twins so this was refreshing.

"More?" She asked as her guest quickly drained the glass.

"Please," Hazel smiled. The MDMA always left her parched. Obviously the fluid from her tongue had travelled to her panties.

The host suffered through small talk for as long as her thirsty old ass could stand. She was paying money to fuck and was ready to fuck.

"So...is she taking the twins place?" She asked in an attempt to set it off.

"Nah she just hanging out with me. She don't get down."

"What! You mean she won't take money to freak with us?" The stud asked incredulously.

"Yes I will! How much?" Hazel heard herself shout. She was slightly embarrassed by the outburst but since it was in the air she left it.

"She pays five hundred!" Sucka-fish blurted so she could keep the other five. The stud worked at a nearby hospital and had plenty of money. She paid good cake for good pie.

"I'll do it," she said standing up. Hazel was so horny she would have made herself cum had the offer not been made. She slipped out of her Prada pants and sat back down.

"Let me see what she talking 'bout" Sucka-fish said and dropped between her legs.

The stud pulled her lacy panties to the side and flicked her tongue across the protruding love button. The other stud moved in close to watch. Hazel was so horny she came quickly and almost caused a scene.

"Oh shit! Did you see that?" The stud shouted when young Hazel's box gushed when she came. It took Sucka-fish a few seconds to reply because she licked the juice from the leather sofa.

"My turn!" The host announced as if reaching the head of the line at six flags. She sucked at the sweet box until it skeeted again only she clamped her lips on those lips and drank straight from the tap.

Hazel kept her legs open for whoever wanted to go again. When she saw Sucka-fish strap up she snapped them closed and protested.

"No! I'm not losing my virginity to that!" She said meaning both Sucka-fish and the big plastic penis.

"I'll give you a thousand dollars if you let me fuck you," The older stud proclaimed.

"I can't," Hazel declined sadly. She mourned the loss of the money but just didn't want the thing inside of her. To both studs surprised she declined when the offer was doubled and tripled.

The two studs had to settle for eating that tender young box. Hazel kept drinking water and juice to hydrate herself then skeet in their mouths.

By dawn when the party finally broke up Hazel went home with two fetishes. Just like her mama she was hooked on drugs and sex. This is how it started, the top of the mountain. It was all downhill from there.

Chapter 6

Sex had been cast in a totally different light after the Tryst with the studs. Touching yourself is not the same as someone else touching you. Days later she could still feel hands exploring and caressing. She could feel the tongue parting her labia and slipping softly inside of her. It made Hazel wonder what a dick would feel like. Her mind flashed to the hunks from back home who offered to deflower her once word got out that she was one of the few remaining virgins. Brad, Conner and Josh all tried to put her as a notch on their belt.

"Damn it!" Hazel fumed seeing her daydreams had made her panties wet before school. The molly she ingested at dawn had her happy as a lark as she changed again.

"As Salaam Alaykum" Fatimah beamed brightly as they both emerged from their homes.

"Whatever," Hazel shot back and looked up the street. On cue a black S.U.V. turned onto the block. "What does that mean anyway?"

"It's actually a prayer, for you. May Gods peace be upon you," Fatimah smiled softly. She could see the changes in the girl already and it was breaking her heart.

Sucka-fish pulled the borrowed truck into the driveway and Hazel jumped in. One of the twins passed her the circulating blunt as soon as her ass touched the leather. She was high enough not to debate about introducing yet another drug into her system. She took it and took a deep drag on the mellow weed.

When the crew got to school the first stop was the grill to order breakfast. Of course they could have gotten a better meal at the hundred other places they passed on the way to school, but who would have seen that. School was about being seen. That's why they all wore name brand fashions, to be seen in them.

"Yall go 'head, I'll be there in a sec." Sucka-fish said when she saw Twan. She made a big production out of handing Eve money for the meal since people were watching.

"Sup Gwen," Twan chuckled when Sucka-fish arrived at him and City-boys designated spot. He knew the stud hated being called by her given name and made it a point to do so as often as possible.

"What's up is I got that sweet young pussy the other night. She's with me, so back the fuck off!" She warned.

"Got? You mean licked. I'ma fuck that bitch! And when I do..."

"She don't want no dick dummy! My client offered three racks to fuck her with the strap and she turned it down. Shawty a virgin and don't want no dick" Sucka-fish bragged.

"I put enough cash in that bitch face and them legs gone spread like butta! Remember I fucked you for what? A number 2 with a coke and a blunt," Antwan laughed.

"Yeah and you put something in my damn coke too!" Sucka-fish moaned. She was still confused about the memory of coming to with him on top and inside of her. What he didn't know was that he got her pregnant that night. She had a lonely abortion and turned to girls after the bad experience. All that remained was an intense hate on a slow boil. It was bound to come to light eventually.

"Only thing I put anywhere was this dick in yo life. And she's next," Twan said plainly.

"Leave her be. She with me," Sucka-fish warned with a deadly glint in her eye. It should have been enough, but Twan just laughed and made it worse.

"Wouldn't mind hitting that again" he said watching her ass as she marched away. It was much to see in the baggy pants and long shirt, but he remembered what was underneath. Still had the pictures of her naked in his phone.

Fifth period math was a class that Antwan really, really needed since he couldn't count well and dealt with a lot of cash. Luckily for him City-boy was almost honest and kept track of incoming and out going monies. He would occasionally round off and keep the change.

The need to learn wasn't what brought him to class today; it was the fact that young Hazel also had the class. It was the only time he would have to catch the girl alone. He paid a girl ten bucks to trade seats with him and made his sales pitch.

"I'll give you five thousand dollars to let me put this in your life." He said pointing under the desk.

Hazel frowned down at his erection and paused from reading him the riot act. First, five grand was a lot of money. Second his dick was short and thin compared to the dick Sucka-fish had. It was about the size of the pink vibrator at home.

"Five thousand dollars," he reiterated feeling the nibble on his line. Twan knew once he got her on his team she would be worth a lot more than his investment. His clients paid well for the little Rachet hood rats he had so this pretty, clean girl would fetch a pretty penny. Plus if she really was a virgin he could sell that cherry at least two or three times. Plus he had a plan to get his money back anyway. He was a slimy nigga with a slimy trick up his sleeve.

"Oh and ole girl told me how much you like getting your pussy ate, so I'ma do that too!" He added.

"Sucka-fish told you that?" She asked incredulously.

"Of course! Said they tried to give you three grand..." He replied seeing she was upset by the breach of trust.

"Ok, give me the money!" Hazel demanded extending her open palm.

"Call me" He said putting his number in her hand. He pulled his penis in and stood to leave. "Five grand, easy money"

~~~~

Hazel made that call later that day. Later that night she was in the passenger seat of Antwan's car heading to lose her virginity. She was going to lose it anyway so why not get a new purse, scarf and shades out of the deal. She was already rolling from her drug of choice when he picked her up.

"I do recall you mentioned something pertaining to oral sex prior to actual copulation?" She reminded. It took him a full minute to process the statement because there were a few words in it that he'd never heard before.

"Oh! Hell yeah I'ma eat that pussy!" He vowed once he translated it to broken english.

She was pleased but truth be told, men eat pussy because men like pussy. Pleasing the woman is nice but being face to face with a vagina is it's own reward.

"Here, this will get you there" Twan said handing her a pill as he drove, Hazel popped it greedily and washed it down with her wine cooler.

"What is it?" She asked after swallowing it down.

"Um...X" He lied. Antwan surmised she wasn't the cheap motel type, not yet anyway, so he took her to a cheap chain hotel.

Hazel was accustomed to five star Hotels when traveling with her wealthy parents. Those days were as dead as they were but she still wrinkled her nose at the generic room.

"Want another?" Twan asked pulling another wine cooler from the bag.

"Sure...and our arrangement? Hazel requested with her hand out. He handed over a stack of cash and filled her cup once more.

Once the cash was counted and cups emptied it was time to get down to the get down. Hazel yawned deeply as she stood to undress. She was blinking rapidly trying to enjoy watching the handsome teen undress. He definitely enjoyed watching her strip off her designer clothing down to her designer bra and panties. She climbed on the bed and laid back.

Antwan intended to keep at least one of his words and crawled between her thick brown thighs. Hazel lifted her hips to assist him in removing her wet panties. He inhaled deeply and savored the clean, fresh smell of the maintained vagina. Eating pussy is like a box of chocolate, you never know what you're going to get. Coming across a neatly trimmed delight made him smile as he leaned in to lick.

"Mmm," Hazel moaned. She was trying to enjoy his quick tongue but the barbiturates he slipped her had her so sleepy. She stayed awake just long enough to skeet I his mouth.

Twan swirled the good P.J 'Pussy juice' around in his mouth for a few seconds before swallowing. He tested to make sure she was under by popping her about the face and head with his little erection.

"And...action!" He announced when he began filming. The show began with him running his fingers in and out of the juicy box.

"Look familiar Gwen?" He laughed toying with her clit. He went on narrated as he pushed inside of her and popped her cherry. The next couple of hours were spent filming the tape rape. His finished off by dictating the hotel and room number. He sent the file to its intended audience then took his money back.

~~~~

Sucka-fish was so mad when she saw the video she could hardly see. She drove in a blind rage ignoring the speed limit along with every other rule of the road to get to the hotel. She bolted up to the second floor and ran down to room 216.

Antwan had left the door partially open but Hazel's legs were cocked wide. Sucka-fish wanted to beat her up too until she saw she was unconscious. She looked at the white fluid ozzing out of her and stuck a finger in it to taste it. She recalled the taste of semen from a recent client call. A husband kept insisting his wife get another girl for a threesome. She finally complied but hired Sucka-fish. She got more out of the than he did. He was expecting some pretty girl to fuck but ended up watching the stud bang his wifes back out. Now the wife hooks up with her once a month.

Sucka-fish was about as fucked up as Twan. She played with the naked girl for a while then went to her car. She returned with a large strap on and fucked her too. Fucked her every which way but loose until she got tired then fell asleep next to her.

Chapter 7

Hazel lay still with her eyes closed trying to figure out where she was and how she got there. There was a blank space in her memory bank along with a throbbing soreness between her legs. She remembered Twan, then the arrangement, the money, the drinks, pill, The Pill!

"You drugged me!" She turned and shouted. Then shouted again seeing it was Sucka-fish laying next to her. "What are you doing here? You guys are in on this together?"

"No! Twan had called...and" Sucka-fish stammered trying to explain. There was no explaining the strap on with traces of virginal blood laying between them.

"Oh my God! You raped me! Both of you raped me!"

Hazel leapt from the bed and scrambled to get dressed. Her overturned purse caught her eye so she ran over to check her money. Not only did Twan take it back, he stole the few bucks she had along with the rest of her molly's.

"You stole my money! The two of you set me up I'm calling my grandfather!" She huffed and stomped out of the room.

Sucka-fish chased her down to the lobby pleading and begging her to calm down. When she yelled words like rape and stolen money it created a scene. People started staring so the stud got in the wind.

~~~~

"Y'all kids something else," Pastor McCoy moaned and shook his head as he drove.

"They just regular kids," Sister Clarice assured him patting his arm.

"Regular kids! I just picked my grandbaby up from a hotel and my grandson floating around like a damn fairy. Britches so tight I bet his little balls hurt!"

Hazel crossed her arms defiantly and Calvin rolled his eyes. He almost told him to talk to the hand but bit his tongue. The reverend was so hurt he didn't even pull all the way into the driveway. The preacher kids took the hint and jumped out. They went inside and the couple went to the church.

Hazel tried to rest but the depression wouldn't let her. The pain and embarrassment of life urged her out of the bed and propelled her down the hall. She entered her grandfathers room went straight for the gun. She put it to her temple, took a deep breath and pulled the trigger.

"I can't even kill myself!" Hazel sobbed. She dropped to the floor and spent the next hour bawling on the floor.

"Un uh, don't let me find out you stressing over some man!" Calvin snapped when he saw his sister moping back to her room. "Chile aint no man worth no tears! Come on let me do your hair. You'll feel much better."

~~~~

Hazel was shocked to see Sucka-fish in her driveway come Monday morning. She had ignored and blocked her every contact attempt all weekend.

"Hey Miss Molly," Sucka-fish smiled as she got out to greet her. The twins both frowned their identical faces up at the thirsty display. "Sup with cha?"

"What is up is that I don't want anything to do with you. You are a rapist and a thief...huh?" Hazel stopped suddenly seeing the badly needed capsules in the stud's hand. She snatched one and quickly swallowed it whole. "I still want nothing to do with you! Come anywhere near me ever again and I'm calling the police!"

The twins really frowned when the stud returned with tears streaming down her face. Sucka-fish slammed the car in gear and tore of down the street. Rage, pain and drugs make a volatile cocktail that can only end in disaster.

"Good morning!" Fatimah sang when Hazel reached the bus stop. By the cheery smile on her face one would have assumed she missed the exchanged. She didn't.

"Why, because you say so?" Hazel snapped like she often does when sober.

"No, because we were given another day to get it right. To stop sinning and draw closer to our Lord." Fatimah stated truthfully.

"What exactly is your faith? What do you believe?"

"We believe in God, his angels, his books, his messengers, the day of resurrection and divine decree. That everything that has happened or will happen was already written."

"I wonder what is written for me" Hazel pondered than stared off into space to reflect.

Hazel felt the effects of the MDMA by the time she got to school. She may have been miserable when she boarded the bus, but was super happy by the time they stepped off.

"Come on let me buy you breakfast" she offered to a confused Fatimah. She guessed by the 360 mood swings she was either crazy or high.

"Just tea please", she agreed and fell in step with her to the cafeteria. "All that stuff has pork in it."

Sucka-fish was breathing fire when she marched into the school. She would have been there already but she made a stop to grab what was needed to do what needed to be done.

"You and ... you and your pork" Hazel chided pausing when she saw Antwan. Obviously rape is pretty funny to him judging by the huge grin spread across his face. Hazel turned her head in the other direction but there was Sucka-fish followed by the confused twins. When she saw Antwan she marched straight over to him.

"Hey lil Miss Molly! This for you!" She called out as she whipped out a large automatic pistol.

Sucka-fish literally wiped the smile off of his face when she fired at it. The slugs made him flip over backwards in his chair. To teach a lesson on hanging with bad company she turned the gun on City-boy. Since he loved to follow Antwan she put two in him and sent him with him. The stud next turned the gun to herself and fired. The bullet flipped her 'A' hat in the air when it came out the other side of her head.

There was a brief WTF pause as people wondered if they really saw what they just saw. When they processed the murder-suicide, panic set in. The crowded cafeteria emptied in seconds as kids fled the crime scene.

"How we 'posed to get money now? How we 'pose to stay high?" Summer moaned.

Hazel frowned at the question but wondered the same thing. How was she supposed to stay high now?

Chapter 8

"You hear that?" Pastor McCoy asked down to Sister Clarice.

"Hmph wmp?" she asked. That's what 'hear what?' sounds like with a mouth full of dick.

"Somebody at the door," he whispered and pulled out of her face. He crept over to his drawer and put six 38 caliber bullets in his old gun. He always kept it unloaded until needed.

The back door opened up just as the Pastor reached the kitchen. He ducked behind the wall, lifted the gun and prepared to shoot. When he saw it was his grandson he debated on weather or not he should shoot the boy.

"Boy what the devil you got on!" He demanded. The boy looked down reminding the pastor that he was naked.

"Um...nothing" Calvin said tugging his short skirt down.

"Get yo ass up to that room!" Grandpa shouted and gave him a kick to get him started.

Calvin took the stairs two at a time hoping his grandfather wouldn't see under his skirt. He was mad enough, no sense making it worse by seeing the thong panties.

"What's going on?" Clarice asked fearfully when the Rev barged in and started getting dressed.

"Damn faggot next door is what's going on! I think he done turned that boy out and I fixing to kill him!"

"No!" Clarice shouted and crossed the room. "We'll call the police in the morning. Better he go to jail then you! You know what they do to pretty boys like you in jail!"

"What?" Pastor smiled at the compliment. He really smiled when she dropped to her knees and showed him.

~~~~

"Surprised you called us," Eve announced skeptically to Hazel in the back seat.

"Why? As much...um, fun as we had all hanging out and um...man do I miss Sucka-fish" Hazel lied. She wanted to get high and had no other avenue except for the twins.

"Well Dante dem don't pay as good as dem dykes, but he got the same good coke," Summer threw in.

"Sounds good," Hazel agreed. She had no idea of what she was getting herself into. Dante was a 300 pound drug dealer and the 'dem' was his ten pound dick.

"Y'all bitches get to it!" He ordered once he led them into his plush apartment.

"Bitches?" Hazel frowned. "I'll have you know..."

"We cool Dante!" Eve cut in. "Can a bitch get a hit or a drink or something?"

"Get to it," he said pointing to a pile of cocaine on the table.

"He crazy so just go along," Summer whispered as her sister leaned in to snort from the pile.

Once she snorted as much as she could her twin did the same. Not wanting to be left out or worse, remain sober Hazel repeated what she saw then do. Dante reached his fat hand out and grabbed her ass when she bent over.

"It burns!" Hazel griped with a grimace. A few seconds later it turned into a smile as the drug seeped into her system. Curiously she leaned back in and snorted some more.

"Aight, aight, get to it!" Dante ordered and hit the remote.

Again Hazel followed the twin's and stripped down to panties and bra. They all danced around allowing him feels between snorts of coke. It was all good until his dick came out.

"What the heck is ....oh," Hazel exclaimed at the sight of the massive meat. It was as long and as thick as her forearm and had a nasty looking vein running through it.

Dante grabbed Eve who was closet and pulled her on top of him. He roughly snatched her panties away and forced his way inside of her. The girl screeched in pain as he slammed in and out of her.

"Come here!" He demanded reaching for Hazel who scooted away. "Bitch get your ass over here!"

"I want some," Summer said to save her sister. He quickly traded twins and gave her the same rough pounding.

Hazel made up her mind that she wasn't doing it. Drugs or no drugs he wasn't putting that inside of her. She leaned in and snorted as much as she could while she could.

"Urgh!" Dante grunted and held Summer in place as he came.

"Let's go!" Hazel urged scrambling for her clothes.

"Hold up bitch! You done snorted up all my shit you gotta let me fuck!" Dante said taking to his feet. The large man crossed the room in a flash and pinned Hazel against the wall.

"Help me!" She pleaded to the twins. Her pleas fell on deaf ears and full noses. Summer and Eve did exactly what she did when Dante fucked them.

The ratchet twins ignored the rape in process and shoveled cocaine up their noses. When the large man forced the small girl to the floor they scooped as much of the coke as they could into their knock off purse and left her.

"Please, please, please don't!" Hazel begged when Dante shredded her panties and tossed them aside.

This wasn't Dante's first rape so he had no problem tuning out her cries for help. Those cries intensified when he squeezed himself inside of her. The tears, whimpers and blood turned him on further. He grunted and came inside the mortified teen. Her ordeal was far from over though. He used his massive weight to keep her place until he recuperated enough to rape her again.

Hazel just gave up after the third time. She actually got up and snorted a few lines of the remaining coke before being raped a forth and fifth time.

"Now if your grimy ass friend's aint run off with my shit I woulda broke you off!" Dante announced once he finally grew bored.

"So how am I supposed to get home?" Hazel demanded.

"The best way you can, now get the fuck out!"

~~~~

"I swear yall kids gone be the death of yall granddaddy!" Clarice said into the rearview mirror to Hazel and Calvin. "You way out here doing God knows what! And this boy here!"

Hazel didn't know what her brother may have done but assumed it had something to do with he glitter in his hair. Pastor McCoy had a pained expression on his face as he drove. His woman noticed first and leaned over to check on him.

"Baby, you ok?" She pleaded. For a reply he let go of the wheel and clutched his constricted chest.

Calvin screamed like the girl he was becoming as Clarice steered the car to the shoulder. Hazel called an ambulance when the car came to a stop.

"He's having a heart attack," one of the paramedics confirmed as they loaded him on a gurney. The family followed behind and waited for news.

"Girl what's wrong with you? You look a mess!" Clarice frowned when she got a good look at the girl in the light. Hazel was shaking, sweating and clenching her teeth from the MDMA and coke.

"I..." She replied and passed out too. When she came to she saw a familiar face looking down at her. "What are you doing here!"

"Calm down chile" The stud said from between her legs. This was the same one who paid Sucka-fish to sex her. "I'm a doctor, and you've been raped among other things. I have to alert the authorizes."

"No! I was with my boyfriend" Hazel replied quickly. She was confused, scared and paranoid from all the drugs she'd consumed so the last thing she wanted to see was the police.

"Boyfriend? Well, he raped you then," the doctor said frowning at the vaginal tears and bruises on her arms and legs. "I'm required by law to..."

"Here," Hazel offered and spread her legs. "You can do what you did before."

The stud doctor frowned at the beat up box oozing blood tinged semen and shook her head. "I'll pass and I'm sorry but I have a duty."

"Ok, and I'll be sure to let them know what you did to me too. Tried to fuck a 15 year old with a big rubber dick!"

"You're 15?" The doctor asked in horror. The last thing she needed was a sex scandal in her life.

"I was when you ate my pussy!" Hazel lied loudly.

"Shush girl!" The stud demanded in a whisper. "I won't say nothing if you don't. But chile what did you take!"

"A molly, a lil coke and wine" she recalled.

"Molly? MDMA? Ecstasy? Are you crazy! That's probably the most dangerous drug on the street. I see kids rushed in here every day from that crap! A few are still here. One is upstairs in I.C.U., two are downstairs...in the morgue!"

"I'm cool" Hazel replied unfazed. Just like her junky mother before her she chose feeling good over common sense. A slave to her desires, just like her mama.

"I hate to introduce more drugs in your system but you need a sedative. Go home, douche, bathe and get some sleep!"

Hazel plucked the pill and popped it in her mouth. She didn't own enough saliva to wash it down but luckily the doctor gave her a paper cup of tap water. When she rejoined Clarice and her brother there was no improvement with grandpa.

"They said to go on home. Nothing more they can do but wait and see." Clarice said sadly. For the first time in years she went to bed without her man.

Chapter 9

Hazel awoke from her coma two days later only to find that her grandfather was still in his. The somber mood in the house only fueled her need to get high. Why stay in a pit depression when you can fly. Oddly enough the daughter of a preacher never once turned to God. Never once dropped to her knees and prayed.

"You got any money?" Hazel demanded barging in on her brother.

"Um...no!" He yelled and quickly tried to switch pages on his computer screen. "My money is my money!"

"What are you up to!" She demanded and marched over to the computer. After a brief struggle for the mouse she overpowered him and clicked back over.

"It's not what it looks like!" Calvin insisted.

"Well it looks like a man with his dick in a young boy's mouth. If it's not that then please, please tell me what it is!" Hazel replied more amused than disgusted.

"Um..." Calvin thought but came up with nothing. He prayed a sick little prayer that she wouldn't click to the next picture but it wasn't answered. "Uh oh!"

"Un uh! Don't run!" Hazel laughed as her brother fled the room. She turned to her brother on the screen and said, "Gotcha!"

Hazel pressed print and hummed as it printed. She emailed the entire file to herself for safe keeping. Money in the bank. She pulled the fresh picture off the printer and marched down the hall.

"Where are you going?" Calvin pleaded trying to block her path. He was too light and she too determined so she shoved him aside. "Still need money!?"

"Your money is your money!" She laughed throwing his own words back at him. They never sound as good as when they come back.

Hazel marched over to the neighbor's house and walked in like she owned the place. She followed her nose and ears into the kitchen where she found Maurice.

"I'm coming out!" He sang in falsetto as he folded a text book omelette.

"I bet!" She laughed startling the...man.

"What the ...I mean what the hell are you doing in my house!" He demanded switching from falsetto to baritone in mid-sentence.

"Oh, I need to talk to you about my little brother." Hazel sang and picked up a slice of bacon and bit it.

"Your grandfather already sent the police over here!" He snapped and snatched the bacon away. "Like Calvin told them I never touched...oh!"

Hazel shut him up by placing the picture on the counter. While he digested the shock of being busted she came around and fixed a plate out of his breakfast. She poured a glass of juice and dug in.

"So what do you want from me?" Maurice crossed his arms and hissed.

"A lot, a whole lot" she laughed, "Oh and this is delicious!"

"Thank you! I use free range eggs and goat cheese an..."

"And I need a few hundred dollars, for starters. We'll negotiate a settlement later" she cut in.

Maurice desperately tore the incriminating pictures to shreds but the chuckled it gave Hazel said what she didn't. This was just his copy. He sighed and removed the cash from his wallet and split it. Money in hand was half the battle but she wanted to get high.

"You guys have all the connections, where can I score some molly?" She asked. Why not, he certainly tell anyone.

"I don't know who that is," he said cracking more eggs for another omlette.

"Not who, what," Hazel laughed. "Ecstasy and coke? Yeah coke too, I like coke!"

"I'm sure they have all that at the club. Hmp, the way they be dancing up in there!"

"What club is this? Can you pick me up some X?"

"Club G.L.S! Only the most progressive club in the city. Gay, lesbian and straight, G.L.S. A pretty girl like you would make a killing down there!"

"Doing what?" Hazel asked lustfully.

"Chile with your body you could dance. Probably make a thousand a night. With that much cash, hell you wouldn't have to black mail people!" He quipped flamboyantly like Calvin had been doing as of late. That would explain where he got it from, that and the limp.

"Girlfriend, you get me in that club tonight and we'll talk about everything else later" she said and polished off the breakfast.

"So what about your brother? Since I'm paying and all..."

"I could care less, just get me in that club!" Hazel announced and walked out.

Chapter 10

"Chile yo granddaddy in a coma and you talking 'bout going out to some party!" Sister Clarice said astonished.

"Like you said, he in a coma so he won't mind," she shot back.

Clarice just shook her head at the curt remark. Now Hazel reminded her of all the shit her mama once put them through. Now standing there with a smirk on her face and hand on hip she looked just like her. The child was lost so she turned to Calvin.

"Boy don't put all that in yo mouth! You gonna mess around and choke!" she warned as Calvin stuffed food in his mouth.

"Oh he can get stuff bigger than that in his mouth!" Hazel laughed and caused him to choke. "Don't believe me I can show you the pictures!"

"I'm sure I don't wanna see no pictures," Clarice replied. It was a guess but she was right, she didn't need to see the boy like that.

"Anyway, holla!" Hazel said throwing up the deuces.

"Come in why don't you?" Maurice said sarcastically as Hazel once again barged in.

"Don't mind if I do. Nice blouse," she laughed at his frilly shirt with its ruffles and bows like the queen of England.

"Wow what a nasty little girl you are," Maurice said shaking his head. If not for a slight resemblance with the sweet old man next door he would have doubted they shared the same blood line.

"That coming from a homo! Just take me to the damn club!" She shot back.

The short ride to downtown was made excruciatingly long by the violent tension. Maurice prayed to what or who he thought was God that the teen would fall over and die but she didn't. He obviously had a little clout at the place since the valet, bouncer and hostess all fussed over him.

"Is Ms. Gene in?" Maurice asked the pretty little young lady working the door. The twenty dollar admission was waved in exchanged for a Hollywood hugs and air kisses.

"Always for you. Go on to his office, I'll let him know you're on the way." She said through a pearly white smile.

Ms. Gene was technically Mr. Gene since he had a penis and testicles. The flaming sissy was waiting at his open door with open arms. Maurice rushed over and greeted him warmly as Hazel blew a bubble with her gum. Just like on the cover.

"And who is this darling little creature?" Ms. Gene fussed when the bursting bubble caught her attention.

"This is the creature I told you about," Maurice replied. He left out all the bitches he called her during that conversation.

"Come on, let's have a look at you," Gene said and ushered them into his office. "Get out of them clothes so I can see what you're working with."

Hazel sighed but complied and striped down to her lacy bra and panty set. No sense being shy now since she was about to dance for hundreds of men, women and mullatos.

"Ooh I have that same set!" Ms. Gene cheered and clapped admiring her under clothes. "You're perfect honey."

Maurice and Gene studied and scrutinized the girl in a purely clinical manner. As one would do before buying live stock.

"How old are you? You look so young, are you sure you're 18?" Ms. Gene asked and gave the correct answer. Had he not gave the legal required age she would have said 16.

"I'm 18, tell him," she said turning to Maurice.

"Um, sure is," he agreed even though her asking him told him she was lying. He could give a fuck so he kept it to himself. Besides, he was naïve enough to believe she would remove her hooks once she brought home some money.

"This is one of the most progressive strip clubs in the city," Gene explained as he gave Hazel the new hire tour. "We cater to Gay, lesbian and straight but often times the lines get blurred."

"How so?" Hazel heard herself ask. She really didn't care but was curious.

"Well, the stages are for each genre but how many times have I seen so-called straight guys watching dicks swinging from the gay stage. Lesbians too, sometime they get so worked up they end up in a V.I.P having gay or straight sex."

"I thought there was no sex in a V.I.P room," she asked.

"Chile they pay five hundred just to rent a room and tip too so I hope so. If you get asked, go in and get him to close his eyes and Ms. Gene will sneak in and take care of him," the sissy laughed. "Think I won't!"

"Oh, I got it" Hazel replied.

"Well, go on in the dressing room and Lashanda will hook you up. Pick whatever you need and you can pay for it at the end of the night." Gene advised and rushed off.

"What I need is some damn molly!" Hazel huffed to herself and walked into the uni-sex dressing room.

"You must be the new girl?" An aging ratchet girl guessed when she walked in. "I'm Lashanda"

"Lashandra can you get me some ecstasy?" Hazel asked cutting straight to the chase.

"Um, I'm sure Snoop would have some. Go on and pick an outfit and I'll grab you a couple," she replied.

"Not a couple, four," she corrected and passed her a hundred dollar bill once owned by Maurice.

While the retired dancer went to retrieve the dope Hazel browsed through a bin full of costumish lingerie. She found a pair of boy shorts and matching bra in a hideous orange. It was bad but it was the best so she slipped into it and a garter.

"Ooh that looks good on you!" Lashanda cheered when she returned. She opened her palm to show Hazel the product and was shocked when she snatched them and swallowed two whole.

"Are you supposed to take that much?"

"I'm a big girl! I missed a few days" Hazel replied.

"Ok big girl. So you dancing for men or women? Only asking so I know what stage to put you on."

"Men I guess, yeah, men" she said feeling naughty.

"Ok what's your stage name and what song you wanna come out to?" Lashanda asked pulling a pen to jot it down.

"Call...me...ooh! Lil Miss Molly! That's my stage name, and anything by Erv-G."

"Aight lil Miss Molly, go mingle, do a couple table dances until the d.j call your name."

"Can I get a drink?" Hazel asked ready to loosen up. "Yup, use the side bar and run a tab, but don't get drunk! Ms. Gene will lose her mind!" The manager warned.

Hazel roamed around the large club looking like a scared deer, a deer in orange boy shorts. She downed her wine and sipped a second glass. When she felt the MDMA invade she began to get happy.

A commotion on a stage caught her attention so she gravitated towards it. A dancer who looked remarkably like Nicki Minaj was putting on. She tossed her hair and swung her fat ass for men clutching fistfuls of money. It obviously rained money because the dancer waded ankle deep. The D.J announced that a hundred more dollars and the shorts would come off causing another flurry of money. The dancer turned, bent over giving a show of ass as the shorts came off. Then men lost their minds at the display but when it turned around they went insane.

"Oh my!" Hazel grimaced at the sight of the dancer's big dick. She kept looking up at its breast then down to its balls.

"I know that girl!" A man announced from the V.I.P section when he saw Hazel. "Nah can't be?"

"Can't be who Dollar Bill?" His hype man asked matching his frown like a good hype man should.

A quality hype man or woman will frown when you frown, laugh when you laugh and co-sign your every action. Validate your every statement. He's a yes man, a flava-flav without the big ass clock. If you don't have a hype man, you may just be one. Yeah boyeee!

The curious baller was about to send for her until the D.J announced her name and she took to the stage. He decided to walk over to get a closer look for himself.

"Her name is Lil Miss Molly!" His hype-man repeated as if his boss some how missed the introduction through the massive sound system. See, you don't have to be too bright to be one.

"For the men who like men we got Big Man swinging his big man on stage one. Ladies, meet Dawn Mist on stage Two and fellas check out Lil Miss Molly out on stage 3." The D.J repeated.

With the happy euphoria that is MDMA Hazel felt no shame as she boarded the stage. Like the saying goes, if you feel no shame then do as you will. Accordingly she began gyrating to the music. A fresh coat of sweat gave her body a sheen that added to her appeal.

The man couldn't get within ten feet of the stage because of the crowd. The name alone piqued curiosity and the pretty, young brown thing confirmed it. Still he was close enough to recall where he knew the girl from.

In fact he knew her parents, watched her grow up. A frown contorted his face as he figured her age. No way could she be old enough to be a stripper. He had to do something, but was stuck watching her work it.

Hazel danced around and allowed men to put cash in her garter. Only the twenties though, you could drop the ones and fives on the ground. Enough was paid for the bra to be removed and show the hard young titties with near black nipples.

The exposed breast caused another flurry of money so that she could come out of those boy shorts. When the price was right she peeled them off too. The sight of her round, brown ass and perfectly manicured box shot hands full of cash in the air. It seemed every man's hand seemed to brush against her vagina when they put money in her garter. The contact combined with the drugs was overwhelming and her stock went through the roof when she bust a nut on the back of a man's hand. His nasty ass licked the juice off to the cheers.

"Send her to the V.I.P room the second she steps off that stage!" The baller ordered a waitress. He used a crisp hundred to punctuate the statement. He paid the bouncer five hudred and went in to wait.

By the time Hazel stepped from that stage all life's plans had changed. Fuck college she had just made over five hundred dollars to dance and cum.

"You got a big baller waiting on you in room B," the waitress announced as hired. "Get that money girl!"

"Say no more," Hazel said sounding like a street savy vet. As she sashayed to the V.I.P she did some mental mathematics. If dude just paid five hundred to get inside of the room he would have to spend at least that to get inside of her. She barged confidently into the room struck a seductive pose then choked. "Reverend Cash!"

"In the flesh," The perfidious pastor proudly proclaimed.

"Wh...wh...wha..." Hazel stammered

"What am I doing here Child I should be asking you that!" he shot back. It sounded sincere and fatherly but his dick was rock hard. He had recalled seeing her at a BBQ at the Sanders house a few years ago. Even as a budding 12 year old she turned him on.

"My daddy and my mama got killed and I'm all alone, and I just started cuz I need money and..." she rambled and turned on the water works.

"Come here girl," the pastor beckoned with open arms. He pulled Hazel down onto his lap and laughed at her expression when she felt the large erection in his pants. "Oh that's just Victor."

"You named your penis?"

"Anything over ten inches needs a name. Twelve inches or more gets a social security number." He explained. He leaned back and pulled it out.

"I never had actual sex before," she said looking at the big dick. It looked more like a fat baby leg then a penis.

The pastor didn't believe her until he reached between her legs. Her vagina was soaked but it still took a little force to insert a finger. He guided her small hand up and down his thick shaft as he played in her pussy. When she gushed in his palm from an orgasm his mind was made up.

"I'm putting you in an apartment. You work for me now" he announced. He wished he had her home now so he could fuck her properly.

"What I gotta do?" She asked with fake trepidation.

"Whatever I tell you to," he advised and pulled her on top of him.

He didn't have the time to try to get inside of her so instead he sat her on his dick and let her ride the outside of his shaft. Reverend Cash gripped Hazel's ass tightly and slid her juicy box up and down. When he growled a guttural moan she jumped up to finish him off with her hand.

"Dang!" Hazel marveled when he exploded sending thick wads of cum in the air. They were so heavy she could hear it land on the leather sofa.

"Go get dressed, I'm taking you home. I'll have an apartment, car and job at the church set up in a couple of days. I have to take my young men's group to Charlotte." He said out of breath.

"Ok!" she sang happily and skipped out of the room. Hazel felt crazy as she entered the dressing room. She was so hot sweat poured from her pores like water. Her vision blurred as her heart rate neared a million beats per minutes.

"Girl are you..." Lashanda began to ask but Hazel fell out before she could finish the question. "Call 911!"

Hazel began flopping around on the ground so violently she injured herself. Her face, head and body were battered viciously as the dancers stood by helplessly. The commotion brought Ms. Gene and others to the dressing room.

"What's wrong with her!" Gene shouted hysterically.

"I don't know!" Lashanda lied. She knew it was possibly due to the drugs she just brought her. What she like most people didn't know is that ecstasy is an extremely dangerous drug. There's no standard formula, which allows makers to put in whatever they like. Some contain Heroin and cocaine along with a host of other chemicals.

Reverend Cash was amongst the spectators. He could only shake his head at the morbid display. When Hazel stopped moving the entire club was eerily quiet.

"Coming through!" A paramedic announced as they pushed through the crowd. They quickly checked for a pulse and loaded her on a gurney.

"One, two, three, four!" the second medic counted along with the futile chest compression. It was just for show because dead people don't need CPR.

~~~~

"Another D.O.A kid, the emergency room nurse said sadly when the ambulance pulled in slowly. There was no siren or flashing lights, no hurry because dead people aren't in a hurry.

"Shot or overdose?" The studly doctor asked.

"Overdose. Picked her up from a club," the nurse replied, and pulled back the sheet so the doctor could make the formal death proclamation.

"Oh no! Oh no," she wailed stumbling backwards. Hazel's face was badly battered from flopping on the floor that it took a second to recognize her. She had lumps and bruises and knocked out a tooth from the beating the floor gave.

"Are you ok? Do you know her or something?" The nurse asked confused by the unprofessional reaction. They saw dead kids everyday in the hospital but she never reacted like this.

"Um, yes...the gentleman who passed away in I.C.U. an hour ago, this is his granddaughter."

THE END

Well, the preacher is dead as is the preachers wife. The preachers daughter now joined her parents. All that is left is the preachers son. Should we go there?